Remembering…

Clifton LaBree

© 2015 By Fading Shadows Imprint

Published by
Fading Shadows Imprint
New Boston, New Hampshire, USA

ISBN-10: 1-943329-31-1
ISBN-13: 978-1-943329-31-1

Cover Design by Vivian LaBree

Dedicated to my wife Pauline, and my family, with thanks for all their support and encouragement.

Chapter One

Joel Thorn leaned against the large gnarled white pine tree that grew out of a crevice in the granite outcrop, listening to the soft whir of the wind passing through the pine needles in the canopy. He could see the looming masses of the northern spur of the Appalachian Mountains that thrust through New Hampshire and Vermont into Maine from his isolated lookout. The sun had just passed below the blue mountain peaks in the distance, saturating them with a red-orange hue. The beauty of the sunset had calmed the anguish that was consuming him. The solitude and the capacity to be alone was a tonic to his soul. The majesty of the sunset filtering through the mountains evoked his love of nature. It was right that he return to this place of renewal.

The panorama was working its magic. He had experienced it often as a young man growing up in rural Maine. He smiled as he remembered how difficult the climb to the lookout rock had been for his mother and father. Those early days of his youth were recalled with a tinge of melancholy. The family had enjoyed picnics at the site. Back then, the trek up to the summit was long and arduous. Now, a roadway was only a few feet from where he had parked his 1941 Studebaker Champion coupe at a pullout from the gravel road. Somehow he liked it better when it was a little more isolated and difficult to get to.

The waning rays of sunshine highlighted the captain bars he wore on his shoulders and reflected off the rows of ribbons on his chest. He was proud to wear the uniform, and he was proud of the men he had trained and led into combat. For the past two years, the company, and the men in it, had been his life. Tears came easy when he recalled, minute by minute, the

1

vicious combat they had experienced in the mountains of Italy. The company had charged ashore to the beaches of Anzio and soon found themselves on the receiving end of massive concentrations of artillery and light machine gun fire. For days they called in supportive arms so that they could move forward. Night and day, the intense enemy artillery continued. They eventually found themselves at a point of physical and mental exhaustion in the foothills of rugged mountain formations. Enemy resistance was heavier than ever.

Orders were received for them to mount an attack against a heavily fortified hill with a monastery built on top. Joel was fully aware that their orders from battalion would mean heavy losses, and with a reluctant heart, he had ordered the company to attack up the hill. The three platoons, one hundred and fifty men, were eager to achieve their objective, the capture of the monastery. They had advanced just a few yards when the entire hillside erupted in explosions. The air was literally filled with hot lead and ragged shrapnel that tore human bodies into shreds of bone and blood.

The company had only gone a few yards when he was lifted off the ground by a burst of machine gun bullets. At first, it made him mad that he could not maintain contact with his men; then, everything went blank. He could recall that he had swallowed a mouthful of black soil when he fell back to the ground. Blood from his wounds saturated the soil forming small rivulets that ran down the hillside. He survived the ordeal, thanks to the quick work of two medics who pulled his riddled body to safety behind a rocky outcrop and administered life-saving plasma into his veins.

Images of the last attack dominated his consciousness. The unspeakable horror of that battle scene was driving him close to the edge of rational thought. He was afraid he was going mad... Out of the one hundred and fifty men he had ordered to the attack, only eighty survived — almost half of his command! How could he explain that fact to the families? Orders were orders and they were meant to be obeyed, but it was him personally that gave the command to attack. Perhaps a different tactic could have been used, or heavier supportive fire could have been called in to soften the area... perhaps... perhaps... The fact remains that he issued the final assault, and he alone had to suffer the responsibility for the results. The company had failed to take their objective, and so did two other attempts. The monastery was finally captured by a Canadian battalion that had been on Joel's right flank.

Tears ran down his face dropping on the rows of ribbons on his chest. He was questioning his competence to command troops again. After treatment in several Army hospitals Joel was rotated back to the states. He had been lucky; his wounds were primarily flesh wounds except for several fractured ribs. His body cavity had been shattered by several bullets that came close to his heart. His spleen had been destroyed, but he was told that a person could live without one. The wounds were deep and serious, but they could be treated with the new miracle drug, penicillin, which halted infection. The Army gave him a short furlough home while his wounds were healing with the warning that he would have to be careful not to do anything strenuous. The Army had recognized that, mentally, he needed the healing powers of familiar surroundings and family.

The chance to be home for a few days was like a dream come true. He was fully aware of his physical and psychological limitations, but he was determined to erase the past. If he could not accomplish that, then the future looked bleak. Sitting against the old white pine tree, taking in the panorama before him, a sense of well-being and peace enveloped him. It was like a tonic to his troubled soul. The beauty of the scene before him was in stark contrast to the images he carried from Italy.

Just as the last rays of the sun were sinking behind the distant mountain peaks, his revelry was broken by the sound of an automobile rapidly climbing the steep roadway. There was a small parking area a few feet from the summit with a deep drainage ditch surrounding it. It sounded as if the automobile had hit the ditch stalling the engine. For a moment there was silence, then the night was pierced by a loud cry of despair that sent chills through his body. Never had he heard such a high pitched scream from a human being.

Joel turned towards the sound of footsteps rushing up the gravel pathway. Suddenly a dark figure could be seen in the limited light running towards the edge of the granite ledge.

He surmised that it was a woman from the pitch of the screams and the long dark hair blowing in the wind. He lurched from his sitting position when he realized that the person was running to jump off the edge into the rocky crevices several hundred feet below! Sobs and painful cries of desperation continued to flow from her lips.

"Stop," he screamed, "You'll go over the edge..." The person paid no attention to his warning.

He was alarmed that a person would wantonly self-destruct in such a gruesome manner as jumping off the precipice. She was too close to the edge for him to grab before she went over, so he tried to stop her forward movement by tackling her around the legs. It was the only option available to him.

He was still recovering from his wounds in Italy, and was not as strong as normal. Thankfully, the tactic worked. His drive to stop her forward movement had knocked her down, but their two bodies were dangerously close to the edge of the cliff which slanted downward. She was fighting, kicking, and scratching with her fists while he was using every ounce of strength to keep both of them from rolling off to oblivion. His weakened condition was not a match for her rage.

Frightened that he might not succeed inspired him to resort to a drastic measure. Freeing his right arm from her ankles, he slapped the woman's face with an open palm. The sound echoed from the hilltop, momentarily silencing her. "My God," he screamed at the top of his lungs. "Aren't there enough dead bodies in this world already?"

Her body seemed to relax. He was afraid he had used too much force, but he was in a situation where he did not have enough strength to extricate their entwined bodies. "Please God, do not desert me now! Grant me the strength to prevent this potential tragedy from happening." His silent prayer was answered in the form of a strong gust of wind from the west that helped to stabilize their position on the lip of the granite. It was like an invisible hand had reached out to push the struggling pair back away from immediate danger.

Renewed by hope, Joel dug his shoes into a granite crevice and rolled the woman's body toward the pine tree. Once there, he paused to rest. She remained unconscious, but they were not out of danger. His major problem was that he doubted if he had the strength to carry her from the lookout to his Studebaker. His body wounds had not completely healed when he was given leave for a few days at home from the Boston Army hospital. He checked for a pulse from the woman. Her heart was beating wildly. He had to do something quickly. Struggling to his knees, holding the woman in his arms like a baby, he slowly, step by step, carried her down the hill to his coupe. Near the coupe, he caught his toe on a raised tree root and fell to the ground, breathing heavily and sweating profusely.

The sudden movement woke her and she began to scream again louder than ever. "Can you hear me, Ma'am?" he shouted into her ear. "I didn't mean to hit you so hard. I apologize if I hurt you. I'm trying to carry you to my car so that I can transport you away from here. Your vehicle is on its side in the ditch and needs to be towed. Can you hear me?"

She began to stir and stopped screaming. A good sign! "Can you walk? I'll help to steady you."

"Why... why did you stop me? Just when I had the courage to jump, you stopped me... why...?"

He could not see into her eyes, but her voice was fraught with pain deep enough that she was willing to end her life with a quick plunge to eternity. He answered her in a calm voice. "Do you realize how painful and permanent your solution would be, not just to you, but to those who love you?"

She laughed and scorned at him. "Are you God or something? Who are you to judge my actions?"

"Would you please get into my coupe? I don't know who you are or why you were so determined to stop your pain, but I can tell from experience that your solution is wrong..."

She allowed herself to be helped into the seat of the small coupe. "You act as if you were an authority on death..."

He snapped back at her flippant remark. "Lady, you may not believe me, but I've seen enough death to last me for a lifetime, and I can tell you that it is never beautiful... Trust me... I'm an authority on death..."

Those words silenced her. She laid her head forward and clasped her face with both hands, quietly weeping. Joel closed the door and walked around to get behind the wheel. "Do you object if I take you to the small infirmary at Lake Holly? They may be able to give you something to ease your pain and despair. Do you understand what I'm trying to say?"

"I hear you," she said with a long sigh of resignation.

Joel started the Studebaker and turned the coupe around heading down the mountain. He was feeling a little dizzy. The winding narrow roadway demanded all of his concentration. He glanced sideways to see how his passenger was doing. She was still holding her head in her hands on her knees. She was the most distraught person he had ever met.

"My name is Joel Thorn. I was born and raised in Lake Holly. I've been away for four years. I always thought that the lookout platform was not very well known by many people. It's a favorite spot of mine. How did you come to know about it?"

"From a friend," she replied between sobs.

It was only a couple of miles from the lookout to the infirmary on Main Street. Joel was struggling to stay alert and just as he pulled into the infirmary driveway, he pleaded to the woman beside him. "Help me, lady, I'm afraid I'm going to pass out!"

She grasped the steering wheel as he applied the brakes and turned off the ignition key. He opened his door to step out and fell to the ground, unconscious...

Chapter Two

Joel had spent countless days in Army hospitals for treatment of his wounds received in Italy and South Africa. They all had the familiar smell of antiseptics. He was disoriented and did not know where he was. His sudden appearance at the small infirmary in Lake Holly caused quite a stir that evening with the nurse on duty and the only physician in town, Dr. Kerr. The kindly doctor knew Joel and his family. He was immediately placed on a stretcher and carried into the examination room where they discovered that two of the large incisions in his stomach and thigh had been bleeding. The stitches had been ripped open by his exertions on the ledge.

A large pool of blood had collected in the seat of his Studebaker coupe. The doctor and nurse immediately began blood plasma transfusions. He was in a coma, and if they had not acted swiftly, he would have died from loss of blood. The doctor could only guess at the extreme trauma of the machine gun bullets to his body cavity. The wounds had partially healed, but the activity on the lookout ledge had opened them again. His uniform was tattered and torn and was covered with blood.

As soon as they had stabilized him, the doctor stitched the incisions, requesting that the nurse call Joel's parents. His condition was still serious. The doctor did not know how much damage had taken place internally, so he called the local fire department to make the transfer to a Portland hospital as soon as possible.

Joel's mother and father and his two younger sisters, Maureen and Sally, arrived at the infirmary soon after the call that Joel was unconscious. His father, Herb Thorn, pulled their 1936 Plymouth sedan beside Joel's Studebaker coupe. Noting that the coupe's driver side window was down, he went to the car, and opened the door to roll the window up. Then, he saw the blood all over the seat.

"My God," he exclaimed, slamming the door shut, turning to his family. "Come, Joel had been bleeding all over his car."

They literally ran into the infirmary in search of information that would quiet their worst fears. Herb Thorn was a short muscular man with dark hair and bushy eyebrows. He was a heavy equipment operator for a construction company. The small community in Lake Holly knew him as a man with a mild disposition and a devotion to his family. Joel had inherited his father's mild manners.

Herb Thorn confronted the nurse at the reception desk, "Linda, what happen to Joel? His car is full of blood. Did someone attack him?" he asked in a wavering voice.

Linda acknowledged the family and embraced Jane Thorn who was close to tears. "Earlier this evening a young woman rushed through the door to announce that a man had fainted beside his car parked at the infirmary. We recognized Joel and began to treat his wounds."

"Who was the woman?" Maureen, Joel's younger sister, asked. She was graduating from high school that spring and was planning to join the Army WACs. "Was she someone Joel knew?"

"The doctor and I have never seen the woman before. We thought she would come to us for she was very disheveled and some of her clothing was torn," Linda told them.

"She just disappeared?" Herb asked with disbelief.

"We don't know, Mr. Thorn. Come, you'll want to see Joel before he's transferred to a hospital in Portland. The Fire Department is sending an ambulance."

The family followed the nurse into the examination room. Joel's color was much improved from when he was first brought into the infirmary, but he had not regained consciousness. The family gathered around Joel filled with anxiety. Sally and Maureen could not contain the tears searching for release. Their big brother looked so helpless and alone. Their fondest memories of him were how he had looked after them when they were younger. They enjoyed hiking in the mountains nearby and bicycling to the coast to go swimming. He was a lot of fun, and they always felt secure with him. They laughed a lot. The girls used to tease him about several girls in his class that had a crush on him. He was shy and was a little bit of a loner, but to his young sisters he was a terrible tease who good-naturedly would accuse them of

9

liking certain boys in town, and he threatened to tell them.

The ambulance arrived to transport Joel. Jane Thorn pleaded with them to let her accompany Joel to Portland. They told her there would be room for her to come along for the ride. Herb and the two girls agreed to stay. They did not have enough gas for the Plymouth to make the round trip to Portland. They were allowed only three gallons of gas per week. When Maureen was fifteen years old, she got a Maine driver's license. She was going to drive Joel's car home where they could clean it up.

In the meantime, the woman Joel had met on the lookout ledge had located a garage that agreed to pull her Ford sedan out of the ditch. Once it was free and nothing was broken, she paid the man and drove down the mountain to a secluded spot near an all-night diner and slept in the car until morning light. She ached all over and was traumatized about the events she had triggered. She was frightened that the soldier was going to die and she was to blame. As soon as the sun rose she drove back to the mountain to revisit what had taken place, trying to make some rational reason for her conduct.

Climbing the pathway up to the ledge from the parking area, she encountered a trail of blood. She cried in horror, forgetting her own problems. On top of the ledge, she noticed two military ribbons and a Combat Infantry Badge lying on the granite near the edge. She picked them up and put them in her jacket pocket. Tears ran down her cheeks. If the soldier dies she would be responsible for his death... Fearful that the police would be after her, she ran back to her Ford, determined to leave town and return to her home in southern Maine.

Joel opened his eyes while in the ambulance and saw his mother bent over him with a worried look on her face. She smiled and took both of his hands in hers. "Where are we, Ma? What's going on?" he asked in a clear voice.

"We're in an ambulance on our way to a Portland hospital. You've been bleeding from your wounds, son. What happened to you? When you left the house this afternoon, you said you were going to the lookout for some quiet contemplation. What happened, son?" she asked in a trembling voice.

He recognized the ambulance attendant and looked at the ceiling of the Packard ambulance, recalling events as best he could. The sequence of events were slow in coming to him, but he could recall the screaming of the woman who wanted to jump off the ledge. The drive down the mountain was vaguely remembered. He was thinking that his seat in the coupe was being soiled by his bleeding incision. After that he drew a blank.

"I'm not sure, Ma. Tell me, how did I happen to be here with you in an ambulance?"

"Linda at the infirmary said that a woman told them you had passed out in the parking lot," his mother told him.

"Who was the woman?"

"No one knows, son. I'm thankful that Dr. Kerr was available to stop the bleeding and revive you with blood

11

plasma. He called the Portland hospital to be alert for your arrival. They're better equipped to take care of you."

"How will you get home, Ma? I have a gasoline voucher from the Army that will get you and Dad more gas while I'm on leave. It's in the glove box of the Studebaker. I hope that I can return home soon."

"As soon as I see that you're settled in at the hospital, I'll call your father to come and get me in your Studebaker. You rest now, son."

The hospital had already called the Boston Army Hospital for a summary of treatment he had received prior to being sent on leave to Maine. The day he arrived was filled with tests and examinations to determine his current condition. Joel's father came later that evening to get his mother. They visited a few minutes.

"Maureen and Sally spent several hours cleaning your coupe, Joel," his father told him. "It sure is a sweet-running automobile. No one in town seems to know who the mystery woman was that alerted the infirmary. Can you add anything to that, son?"

"Nothing, Dad." He believed that it would be better if she remained unknown. It would be difficult for him to give a coherent account of what took place on the ledge. Even now, he was uncertain about the chronology of events. The mystery lady would have to remain that — a mystery. The people in town may talk and amplify on the facts, but it would soon die down. The war news dispelled all other events in small towns across the country.

The next morning after his mother and father returned home, he was given a letter addressed to him left at the information desk at the hospital. There was no return address and no postage mark on the envelope to show where it was mailed. Joel was curious and opened the envelope to read:

May 15, 1944

Dear Captain Thorn;

I owe you an expression of gratitude, an apology, and an explanation for my conduct.

The first is easy for me. Thank you for being on that ledge when I was depressed enough to want to end my life. Thank you for interceding when it meant endangering yourself. Your response to my action has been a frightening revelation for me. I can now admit to myself, to you, and to my God that my irrational behavior violated His will and the sanctity of life. I'd give anything to erase the sordid act and the unfaithful conduct that made it seem like the only solution available to me…

How do I tell a complete stranger what took place in my life that brought me to the brink of self-destruction?

It has generated a lot of soul-searching on my part. In doing so, I came face to face with my own frail constitution and failures. It was not a pretty picture! May God forgive me for giving in to elemental human weaknesses. I was engaged to a wonderful young man who went off to war right after Pearl Harbor. We had planned to marry as soon as it was over. That was February 1942 when he left to join the Army Air Corps.

For a long year I wrote a letter almost every day to him, even as an old acquaintance worked diligently to get me to go out with him. At first, I refused, but his efforts were relentless. Finally, I gave

13

in to his wishes. To make a long story short, I became pregnant. (Oh, God, I can't believe I'm confessing this to a total stranger... Please forgive me!) When I told my friend of my condition, he left town to leave me to live with the consequences of my betrayal.

In order to protect my fiancée from knowing about my unfaithfulness, I had an abortion done by a back-room quack who got the evil act done without complications. Not long after that, we received word that Donald, my fiancée, was killed in action. His B-17 Flying Fortress was shot down over Germany with no survivors.

I am a teacher who has worked hard to instill and inspire students beyond their dreams. How phony my personal life proved to be in comparison... May God forgive me for my actions...

I am enclosing the Combat Infantry Badge and two ribbons for a Silver Star and a Distinguished Service Cross I found when I revisited the ledge the morning after. You have proven to be a very brave soldier, and I can't apologize enough for what happened. Your presence, your courageous act on the ledge, and your devotion to our country have been an inspiration for me. With God's help, I hope to be a better person from the one you slapped in the face.

May God watch over you, Captain Joel Thorn. Your name was in the local newspaper today. I'm relieved that they took you to Portland for treatment. How does a person say "Thank You" for saving their life and giving me the courage to start anew?

Forgive me. I'll pray for you.

The mystery lady who shattered your solitude

Chapter Three

The letter left Joel with a little more of an understanding of why and how the occurrence on the ledge took place. His natural curiosity was left unfulfilled with the letter because the lady remained an unknown. He could accept that, but it left a big question mark in the deep recesses of his consciousness. Some time, when the war was over, he'd try to locate who her friend was that showed her the ledge area. That person held the key to identification and the closing of the incident.

The Army was concerned about his care and ordered him to be evacuated to Boston via plane. Joel's furlough home was terminated by the Army officials. They were responsible for his rehabilitation; therefore, they wanted to be in control of his treatment when care was needed. The family was saddened by the move from Portland, but they were encouraged that the Army's track record rehabilitating wounded veterans was beyond compare. He was in good hands.

Joel arrived in Boston by way of a Naval transport out of the Naval Air Base at Brunswick, Maine. As soon as he arrived the Army gave him the most thorough physical examination he had ever experienced. He was immediately restricted to limited exercise until his wounds were completely healed. His wounds had become infected, which brought his temperature up. The new miracle drug, penicillin, was administered on a regular basis. Within a few days, his temperature was down to normal.

The magnitude of the wounds some of his fellow soldiers had to deal with staggered the imagination. Joel mingled freely with them. Their bond of fraternity was real and long-lasting. An Army hospital in time of war, regardless of its location, is the concentrated center of more pain and suffering than any hospital in the world. Hot steel fragments inflict horrible damage to the fragile human body. Broken bodies were sad enough to contemplate, but those brave soldiers who had emotionally slipped from reality were the most pathetic and required the most attention. Many would be lost forever to society... Their brethren who suffered with them knew first hand that the price of freedom is high.

Yet, as horrifying as the wounds are, the morale and spirits that prevailed in most of the wards was high — a tribute to the tenacity of the American soldier. No one suffered alone. Those who had suffered the most or were feeling the worst, experienced the uplifting joy and camaraderie of brothers who circled their wheelchairs and crutches around those in doubt to show that they were not alone. Self-sacrifice and courage were a daily phenomenon within the wards, frequently more than was shone on the battlefield.

One month after Joel returned to Boston, his older sister Maureen and an old classmate of Joel's, Inger Williamson, rode the Boston and Maine train from Lake

Holly to Boston for a visit. Inger was a second generation Swede immigrant with blond hair and blue eyes. She came from a farm family living near the Thorns. Joel and Inger had dated often during their years in high school. She had a reputation of being a hard worker and had a large circle of friends. Whenever the class sponsored musical events or plays with local talent, Inger was a diligent worker and was primarily responsible for the class to raise enough money to spend a few days in Washington. It was a trip they all remembered and talked about later in life.

Joel hardly recognized his sister Maureen. She had grown into a young adult with confidence and grace. Her brown hair was cut short close to her ears. She was anxious to join the Army now that she had graduated from high school.

"My, it's nice to see familiar faces," Joel greeted them, sitting in his wheelchair beside the hospital bed. He hugged them both enthusiastically. "Why don't we go out on the balcony where we can be more private?" He pointed the way down through the ward.

Whistles from the admiring soldiers accompanied them to the balcony. Maureen and Inger smiled and waved back at the men. Soldiers traditionally are attracted to pretty girls. "The guys are envious of me," Joel exclaimed, carefully getting out of his wheelchair to support himself against the balcony rail.

"I see that you're able to move about, big brother. That's encouraging news," Maureen said, noting that the deep lines around his mouth and eyes that had worried the family when he was home for a few days had diminished. "Inger is attending normal school here in Boston."

"That's great, Inger. You'll make a great teacher," he replied honestly.

She smiled at him. "You flatter me, Joel. When we graduated four years ago, I thought I wanted to do secretarial work, but it was not for me. I've got a few more courses to finish this summer and I'll have my teaching certificate. The school is over on Boylston Street. It would be nice to visit an old friend. I didn't know you were here until I spoke to your mom."

"I'd enjoy that, Inger. I think often about our good old days in school. It helps to get away from some of the bad memories that goes with being a soldier."

"The Army wants me to report to the nearest recruiting station next week for boot camp," Maureen proudly announced.

Joel chuckled, "I hope it's a lot easier for you than my boot camp was at Fort Devens."

Joel was dressed in pajamas and an Army robe with slippers on his feet. It was warm in the sunshine with a soft breeze blowing across Boston Harbor. It was filled with ships of every description. An Army medic approached Joel with a glass of water and medication. "It's time for your penicillin again, Captain. Since it's such a nice day, and you have the luck of being accompanied by two lovely ladies, the doctor told me you could leave the hospital for a few hours providing you don't overdo. A moderate amount of slow walking will do you good."

The announcement brought a smile to Joel's face. "That sounds great. The three of us could go out to eat. I understand there's an officer's mess close by the hospital. I'll be the envy of every soldier we meet."

Ten minutes later, he was dressed in the proper summer tan uniform being wheeled to the entrance portico where Maureen and Inger were waiting for him. "Enjoy your break, Captain. Just don't get too tired. Use your cane to steady yourself," advised the friendly medic.

With Maureen and Inger at his side, they slowly walked one block to the officer's mess. It was mid-day, and the club was not too crowded. Later towards evening, it would become a pulsating haven of boisterous men from all the services. The three of them entered and slowly went through the buffet line, amazed at the wide selection of foods available. They all chose macaroni and cheese and ham with a salad and coffee. Desert could come later. Maureen offered to hold Joel's cane while he made his selections.

They sat at a window looking out at the Dorchester Heights National Monument overlooking the Boston Harbor. Joel had always been a history buff, and he gladly related the significance of the location. "In the early days of the Revolutionary War, General Washington ordered a Colonel Knox to retrieve the cannons captured by militia units from Connecticut, led by Benedict Arnold, and Vermont, led by Ethan Allen at Fort Ticonderoga on Lake Champlain. They dragged the cannons over the ice and snow to be positioned at Dorchester Heights where they could neutralize the armed British ships in the harbor. After a significant bombardment, the British left Boston Harbor for Nova Scotia, allowing Washington to move the Continental Army south to counter any moves by the British at New York."

Inger had listened with a pensive look on her face, studying the terrain out the window. "And now we are at war again..." she said almost in a whisper.

Joel heard what she said and quietly picked at his salad. "By the way, does anyone in town know the woman I met at the lookout?"

Maureen shook her head. "Not that I've heard. The whole town is talking about her and wondering who she is."

"The garage owner, Jake Higgins, said he'd never seen her before. She was very distressed when he pulled her Ford automobile out of the ditch. No one ever got her license plate number either. More and more, she's becoming a mystery woman. Everyone has their own version of what she was trying to do," Inger added. "I feel sorry for someone that is so depressed they'd choose such a ghastly death."

Joel remained silent about the letter he had received from the woman. The letter explained her conduct, but did not give a clue as to her identity. The deception still bothered him.

They left the officer's club and took a cab ride around Boston to the Bunker Hill Monument and past the school and dormitory in which Inger was staying. Maureen was planning to stay with Inger at the dormitory and leave in the morning on a train back to Maine.

Ever since the war started, every community located on the eastern seaboard adhered to blackout regulations. No lights could be visible from the outside of any buildings. Blinds had to be drawn or lights turned off. Automobiles had to have the upper half of their headlights and taillights masked with black tape. Joel had been advised to return to the hospital before blackout time.

The girl's visit had been a welcome diversion for Joel. Every day was the same in the hospital, but he was improving, and he did not complain. He admitted to them that he was a little tired. The cab stopped under the portico entrance where both girls saw him to the door. Maureen warmly embraced him.

Inger did the same. "You take care, soldier. It's nice to see you again. I'll be by to visit as often as I can. Goodnight, Joel."

He kissed her on the lips. "Thanks for the visit, Inger. I'll look forward to seeing you again." He waved as they got into the taxi.

The next day Maureen stopped to say good-bye again just before her train left for Maine. It was a sad moment for both of them. She was about to leave for the Army, and he would soon be returning to active duty. With the war raging across the oceans there was no guarantees for tomorrow; there was just today. Uncertainty and anxiety filled the hearts of every family member who had loved ones in the armed services. It had become a way of life.

It was a tearful parting for Joel and Maureen. His younger sister had become an adult almost overnight.

She clung to him for several minutes. Finally, she held him at arm's length and said, "Thanks for being my big brother, Joel. I'm so proud of you. How nice it was to grow up in Lake Holly where all of my friends thought you were so handsome, especially in your uniform."

He grinned at her. "Flattery will get you anything, Sis. You have my service address. Be sure to send me yours as soon as you arrive at your basic training depot. When I leave here, probably by the end of summer, I'll forward my new duty station."

"Tell me before I leave." She asked with a smile, "Will I as a private have to salute my officer brother when we meet?"

"Always, Sis," he teased her. "Now go and take on the world, Maureen. You'll always be in my prayers."

"And you're in mine, brother."

He waved as her cab disappeared in the morning traffic. Suddenly he felt alone and sad. That night, he laid on his cot and stared at the ceiling. His head was filled with sweet memories of better days in his youth. Mixed with those were images of men he had lost in combat. The two were intertwined. Sometimes he wondered if he was going out of his mind. Inger's presence had triggered memories of their relationship. The two of them dated each other all through the school years, and, on occasion, they both dated someone else with no guilt feelings of betrayal. They were never a "steady couple" like some of their friends.

Joel and Inger knew each other well enough to know their favorite songs, movies, and books. It was an easy relationship that each felt comfortable with and asked for nothing in return. His view of Inger, his best friend in town, began to change when they took the senior class trip to Washington, D.C. There they visited all of the attractions such as the Washington Monument, Lincoln Memorial, and the Tomb of the Unknown Soldier. They even had a visit to the office of Senator Margaret Chase Smith from Maine. It was an impressive trip for a class such as theirs from small town America in 1940.

At the Tomb of the Unknown Soldier, they had watched the Army's Third Regiment conduct a precise and solemn change of the guard. It was a moving sight that brought tears to their eyes and lumps to their throats. Inger had grasped his hand and held it tightly during the ceremony. When it was over, she had embraced Joel and whispered in his ear: "I don't know what I'd do if anything happened to you."

It was a poignant moment for both of them. The whole world was in chaos with the threat of war on the horizon. Joel's decision to join the Army added to the potential for disaster. Shortly after high school graduation, Inger came to his house to say good-bye to him. He was just placing his suitcase in the faithful Plymouth. "Good morning, Inger, I was hoping to see you."

She had been crying and was conscious that he would know. "I wanted to say good-bye to you and to wish you luck. There are a lot of people in this town that are very proud of you, and that includes me. I'll write to let you know all the gossip and other stuff going on. I understand how important letters are to soldiers away from home. My father said they were all that kept him from going crazy in the last war."

"That will be nice, Inger," he had replied. "I leave this little town with warm memories for all the good times we've had. Your friendship has been special over the years. I'll miss you." He had embraced her for a long time wondering if he had made the right decision.

"I'll wait for you if that is what you want," she told him in a soft voice. "These are terribly unsettled times, and no one knows what the future will be, but I want you to know that I'll be here for you no matter what."

The sincerity of her promise touched him, and he kissed her on the lips. She released him and slowly walked away filled with a deep sense of discovery and of loss.

Chapter Four

Early in the morning of June 6, 1944, Joel was taking a shower when the entire hospital floor erupted into cheers, whistles, and shouts of joy. Something big must have happened, he thought, rushing to dry himself and bandage his wounds which were healing rapidly. Someone opened the door and yelled: "The allies have invaded Europe, landing at Normandy."

"Ah," he cried aloud. The big push against fortress Europe was underway. He rushed to his ward where the patients were gathered around a radio set up in the center of the room, listening to descriptions of the invasion force. The euphoria he felt at that moment was beyond description. This event in history was possible because of the courageous actions of everyday Americans who joined up to serve for the duration. The actions of men such as his company in Italy had made this monumental day possible. At last, their sacrifices had been validated! He was proud to be an American.

When Joel first joined the Army in June, 1940, four years ago, it was nothing more than an armed constabulary force incapable of even defending the country if they had to. Men, supplies, equipment, and trained leaders were desperately needed to build an army capable of defeating the Germans and the Japanese, two of the most powerful military nations in the world at the same time. It was a daunting task ahead of the United States, but typical American ingenuity and industrial capacity astonished the world with their ability to adapt to changes in a hurry. Joel had doubted the Nation's ability to recover so quickly.

His first posting in the Army after boot camp was that of a squad leader with corporal stripes stationed at Fort Benning, Georgia, the Army's largest infantry training center. They specialized in training officer candidates to command small units such as companies, battalions, and regiments in the new Army that was beginning to take shape all across the country.

One day after a grueling march in the brutal Georgia heat, he was asked by his regimental commander, Colonel Wason, if he would be interested in applying for Officer Candidate School. The Colonel was a West Point graduate who saw promise in the young corporal. Joel was elated and told him he'd like to apply, but he only had a high school education and was doubtful if he would be selected. Colonel Wason told him that the only abilities an officer needed to command troops in combat were a reasonable amount of intelligence and a good dose of common sense. The two virtues required were integrity and character, and no one can teach those in a classroom. He never forgot that short definition of an Army officer.

He anxiously applied and was accepted to be a part of the next class to be processed at Benning. He had found that several Dutch and Canadian soldiers were in the class as well as several men from the Marine Corps. It proved to be an intense three month course. The title, "ninety day wonder" was readily applied to all of the graduates by the rest of the Army. Joel had never worked so hard in his life. He studied movements of troops of various sizes and learned how to develop coherent simple orders under adverse conditions that answered what, when, where, and how. Much time was spent on tactics in the field, but they were warned that once in actual combat, ninety percent of their time would be devoted to logistics, ten percent to tactics. They all doubted the statement, but soon found it to be true.

Discipline, morale, and success in combat all began with the officer in command. Joel had a natural trust and respect for the American infantryman. Respect always came from the top before it filtered down through the ranks. There were no bad battalions, only bad commanders. Some officers shouted and barked their commands to show the men who was in charge. Orders were meant to be obeyed. Joel had a knack of conveying orders in a civil manner with a clear understanding of why they had to be carried out. He wore the responsibility of command with grace and firmness. He worked diligently to develop a rapport with the men. That kind of a two-way relationship developed higher morale and success in carrying out a mission.

He was well aware of the dangers of getting too close to the men. It could mean a more difficult emotional experience when losses were taken, and it could develop a tendency to avoid risk which could be disastrous in combat. The young soldiers, many fresh from high school, looked to him to not only lead them in combat, but to always have their best interest at heart. He took that responsibility very seriously.

The company he had in Italy was made up of a typical slice of Americana. Young boys who became men in seconds after their introduction to fire from the enemy. Joel had worked hard to see that mail was delivered as often as possible and that hot meals and coffee were distributed timely when they were not on the front lines or attacking. The men deserved all the care they could get. He was like a mother hen looking after their needs. He made himself available to the men and listened with a sympathetic ear to their concerns. That contributed to what the Army called cohesion. Those units that had that feeling of unity were the best in the Army. Being "one of the boys" was never his aim, but that did not mean he had to be a stranger to them. He associated himself as one of them even though he wore the higher badge of rank.

The down side to it was the level of trauma he experienced ever since he left Italy to recover from his wounds. The physical aspect of the wounds did not bother him that much. Proper medical care would soon heal them. The emotional load was a different story. It was the images of eighteen-year-old men being torn to pieces by steal projectiles that kept him awake nights. Was that the price he would have to pay for being too close to his men? He was never able to answer the question, and was unwilling to change the way he handled his command when he returned to combat. The heavy losses were a part of the burden he shared with every other combat veteran in the U.S. Army. Any citations he might earn were accepted in the name of those he left on the field of battle where he collected their dog tags. He had reconciled that that was the price he was willing to pay as long as they led to victory.

His introduction to combat came when he led a platoon of forty men across the beaches of North Africa November 1942. All the lectures he had attended could not prepare him for the physical and emotional impact. It was part of his introduction to war that he had to experience personally. After the initial shock, he developed a "what the hell" attitude that served him well. He insisted on leading from the front where he knew what was going on. That leadership decision helped to cement the relationship and the risks he shared the same as the men. His actions spoke louder than words. He gained a reputation of running a crack outfit with a minimum of gripes or complaints.

At the end of combat operations in North Africa, he was given a field promotion to Captain and command of the company which his platoon was a part of. They fought all across Sicily to the mainland at Messina where they were pulled from the battle line and trucked to a rear area for some much needed rest and relaxation. The company then received replacements and replenishment of their weaponry and mobile capability. Joel received a brand new International Half-track which he converted to a command vehicle with radio links to every platoon in the company. He mounted two fifty-caliber machine guns on the bed of the truck. Whenever they were on the road in an attack mode, he rode second behind the point Jeep.

An Army company kept the administrative records of every man in the unit. They also had field kitchens for their own mess. Joel ordered the company cooks to maintain coffee and sandwiches twenty-four hours a day. That attention to detail was not lost on the men. He was the most popular officer in the regiment. The solidarity and support he received from the men was comforting. He reciprocated their respect and admiration, looking upon his position as a privilege instead of a right.

Pandemonium broke the normal silence of the Boston Army Hospital. It was the sixth of June, 1944, and the Allies had just crossed the English Channel with a massive military force to destroy the German war machine and to drive the Germans back to their own country. When the hospital inmates learned of the operation, shouts and screams of joy filled the hallways. Joel was taking a shower when he heard the noise. Something big had happened. He shaved and dressed in a clean tan uniform of the day and joined in the festive occasion.

He was getting stronger and feeling better by the day. The doctors had removed the last of his stitches and were pleased with his recovery. "When will I be able to report for duty?" he had asked the doctors.

"You were a lucky soldier, Captain. The same number of bullets that entered your body cavity could have killed you instantly if they had deviated slightly from their trajectory. To answer your question, I'd be willing to sign your release within two weeks from now," the head surgeon told him.

"Do I have to stay in the hospital that much longer? Seeing the severity of the injuries that some of the soldiers have makes me almost feel guilty taking room when someone more in need could use the bed," he replied.

The doctor grinned, "Would you like to go home for two weeks?"

"I was hoping you'd offer that option to me, Doctor. I can relax and do my workouts better at home than here."

"Let me put it this way, Captain. I want to monitor your recovery for a little longer, maybe two more days; then, I'll discharge you until the end of June. By that time you'll receive orders from your normal chain of command. I will reserve the right to fill out your final fitness report at the end of the month. How does that sound, Captain?"

"I agree with your proposal, sir. The wounded guys in this hospital have inspired me and given me hope for the future. There was a time in early 1941 when I did not feel the same."

The doctor studied this serious soldier before him. "This country is blessed with courageous people who have risen to the desperate challenge the country faced. This is a heart-wrenching war to have to experience, but it has given all of us a reason to be proud to call ourselves Americans. How proud we are of the men and women who have so valiantly resisted and defeated the evil that threatened all of society as we know it."

"I could not have said it better, Doctor."

31

The day before he was scheduled to leave for Maine, Inger paid him a visit. "Classes are over for a few days until the next semester, so I thought I'd come over to see how Lake Holly's favorite son is doing," she smiled, kissing him on the cheek. She was wearing a light blue dress with a dark blue blazer and a small beret placed at an angle on her head. She received whistles as she walked into the ward and happily waved back at the soldiers.

"Thanks for coming, Inger. I have some good news to share with you. I'm being released tomorrow. I have a furlough home until the end of the month."

"That's wonderful. I was going home tomorrow, also. There's a great movie playing at the theatre on Mass. Avenue, *Going My Way,* with Bing Crosby. I was hoping I could take you out this afternoon," she explained with a happy air of expectation.

"I'd like that, Inger. I'm in a lot better condition than when we went out with Maureen. When we get home, I'll be able to drive some, too. The Army has issued me a gas clearance card."

They left the hospital on the waterfront and leisurely walked to the theatre near the intersection of Boylston Street and Mass. Avenue. Both of them were glad to be together. Inger confided in Joel that she was very homesick when she first moved to Boston. The big city was unfamiliar and so impersonal. Masses of people going and coming in endless numbers made her feel even more alone. Their small town of Lake Holly was totally different. It was impossible to go into the small village without meeting someone you knew.

"When I left for the Army it was the first time I was away from home, and I was homesick, too. It really was bad for me surrounded with strangers. We were not allowed to receive mail or phone calls for the first two weeks. Most of the men experienced the same thing. Some refused to admit it, but we all knew better," Joel said.

The movie was a wonderful experience for both of them. For two hours they were able to forget the war and the toils around them. They walked out of the theatre into the bright sunlight. Inger had insisted on paying for the tickets because she had asked him out. He conceded reluctantly. She smiled and told him that she had just gotten a check from her work in the dormitory cafeteria where she worked every morning and evening.

"Now," she asked, looking into his eyes. "Are you okay to walk, or do you want to call a taxi? We could eat at a good restaurant near the waterfront that serves seafood. It isn't very far."

He was pleased to see her expressing a little more independence than was normal for her. She was growing up, and it was becoming. "I'm strong enough to walk, Inger. Fresh seafood sounds good to me. I haven't had fried clams in ages. I'll agree on one condition, young lady. I make a larger salary than you do, and I want to pay for dinner. Your generous offer to take me to the movies is appreciated. Now dinner is on me, okay?"

She playfully kissed him on the cheek and linked her arm in his. "Okay. How nice it is to be with you, Joel. I've missed you a lot since you left for the Army."

Chapter Five

They sat at a waterfront restaurant watching the ships in the harbor. Joel studied Inger's quiet acknowledgement of the warships and their significance in the future the two young people faced in a world clawing each other apart. There was a pensive, even a solemn, air about her today that made him feel that he was seeing her for the first time as an adult instead of a classmate. She always had a quiet, reflective personality. In school she was always on the honor roll. Joel admired her for that accomplishment, but, at times, he was piqued at her because he had to struggle for good grades. She got along well with friends and classmates in school, yet there was always that illusive part of her that defied definition.

Now, four years later, he saw those same mannerisms and traits of character in her. He knew from experience that a beautiful scene such as a colorful sunset or sunrise could bring tears to her eyes. At times, he was never sure what she was thinking. One of their classmates, who was Inger's best friend, eloquently defended the mood swings they had experienced with her: "My dear friend, Inger, is a little bit of a dreamer. Perhaps, when she grows older, she'll be a little bit eccentric, but she will leave us with a rich legacy of kind acts of friendship and generosity. Loveable eccentrics have left this world better than they found it. Inger will always have my respect and friendship."

Inger knew that Joel was studying her. "I see all those ships in the harbor, and they remind me that one of them may be the ship that carries you away from us and to the battlefield. I'll be relieved when this horrible war ends."

"I speak as an authority, Inger. No one hates war any more than the soldier that fights it," he said. "I was watching you, and for a moment, I knew you were not here with me. I've occasionally seen that expression in you ever since we were kids."

"Are you criticizing me or giving me a compliment?" she asked with a smile. "I apologize if my serious side gets the best of me at times."

He reached across the table grasping her two hands in his. "Oh, no, Inger. I was not being critical or complaining. Don't ever apologize for being who you are. I have a feeling that the children in your class when you become a teacher are going to be lucky kids."

The compliment brought a tear to her left eye and slowly ran down across her cheek. She deftly wiped it away. "Thank you for telling me that, Joel. All through our school years I considered you my best friend. Those few times when I gave in and went out to a movie with a friend, I could only wish that it had been you. There has never been anyone that made me feel that way. I hope I'm not stepping out of line, Joel. These uncertain times demand that we be honest with each other and ourselves.

I've been thinking about this ever since you left for the Army. Maybe you could read between the lines in the letters I sent you just how I felt." She caught her breath and continued.

"I'm going to be bold and honest with you today, Joel Thorn. I love you and I want you to know that it is not a fickle infatuation or a fantasy dream. It's important to me that you completely understand that my declaration of feelings does not in any way place an obligation or any commitment on you. Friendships are a precious gift from God, and I've treasured ours more than you realize. Are you angry that I'm so candid with you at this time?"

Throughout his adolescent years, Joel had sensed that Inger had deeper feelings for him than was reciprocated. She never pushed her feelings on him, keeping them to herself. After he joined the Army, she faithfully wrote several times a week. They were filled with up-lifting chatter of events and people in town, and were a ray of sunshine in his life. He wondered now if he had been selfish with her or taken her for granted. He was certain that his answer to her declaration would have a powerful influence on their relationship from this day forward. He prayed for the right choice of words.

"Your feelings have not been a secret, Inger. Over the years I've been aware of what was in your heart. You must believe me when I tell you that I am privileged to be the object of your affections. How lucky I am. The question is where do we go from here?"

"I never intended to put you in a position where you have to declare yourself, Joel," she quickly responded.

"Nobody can ever know what you've been through already, or what awaits you when you return to duty. These explosive times are not conducive to specific long range plans. I simply wanted you to realize that no matter what you do or where you go, there is someone at home who cares for you. Please don't make it anything more than that. We've always been friends, and I, too, have cherished that.

"At some other time and place, if your feelings are the same as mine, then we can make plans for the future. Don't agonize over this, Joel. You've made a commitment and taken a solemn oath to defend this country we all love against our enemies. That is a monumental task that should have a priority on your heart and soul." She kissed his hands.

In that moment of devotion, he admired her unselfish generosity. She had made it easy for him, but she was correct. There would be time for relations once the war was over. He was relieved of a difficult choice that could have hurt the gentle lady, and she did not deserve to be hurt. They slowly walked back to the hospital where they agreed to meet in the morning for the train to Maine.

He kissed her and looked into her dark eyes. "Thanks for being you, Inger. Keeping things on this level for now is a comforting course. I'll sleep better tonight knowing that I have your support. Until tomorrow morning, old friend."

"Until tomorrow, Joel."

Joel began to get stronger by the day once he was back in familiar surroundings at Lake Holly. He got up early in the morning and walked to the village center and returned every day, a distance of about two miles. One day he walked in the opposite direction south towards the road leading to the lookout rock. He had overextended himself by going twice as far as planned. Half way back the rural mail carrier, Acer Kimball, stopped to give him a ride. Joel was relieved to climb in the back seat of the Model A Ford. The front seat was always filled with mail.

"I heard that you were home for a while, Joel," Mr. Kimball acknowledged him. He was a small man with delicate features normally seen with a corn cob pipe in his mouth. Most of the time it was not lit. He had retired from the Postal Service prior to the war and agreed to take on his old job for the duration once the young men from town began to join the armed forces. His only son, Joseph, was in Joel's class in high school.

"It's good to be home, Mr. Kimball. Have you heard from Joe lately? We kept in touch with each other until I went to Africa. I always envied the way the Navy served regular meals on board ship. Our cold C-rations were a poor substitute."

"The last time we were certain about his whereabouts his destroyer had passed through the Panama Canal on its way to the Pacific. I served in the Navy during the last war. Joe felt the same about the Navy as you did about the Army, Joel. We heard about your promotions to officer rank. It has made us all proud."

"I was lucky, Mr. Kimball," Joel replied. "I want to stop in to see the Hilton family while I'm home. Their son Bob was my best friend in school. His death on Guadalcanal has been difficult to accept."

"They've had a rough time ever since the bad news arrived. We all pray for the killing to end. Well, Joel, here we are at your door. Your family has some mail," Mr. Kimball said, handing him a packet of letters. "You take care, Joel. We're praying for you and all the boys from town."

"We all realize that, Mr. Kimball. Thanks for the ride. Tell Joe I'm thinking of him. Goodbye."

"May the Lord take a liking to you, son."

Joel smiled at the kindly ways of the aging mail carrier. Sweat began to run down his forehead. He had been too anxious and had over extended himself that morning. The Army doctors had warned him to use moderation in returning to normal.

Joel's mother saw him climb the steps onto the porch. "You look tired, son. I've got a pot of coffee on the stove in the summer kitchen." Her summer kitchen was a portion of the utility room between the main house and the shed leading into the barn. His father had installed a kerosene stove for cooking so as to not heat up the whole house in the summertime. Occasionally the burners had to be cleaned, or they would smoke too much.

"I'd like a cup of coffee and some of your boulla rolls, Ma. I used to dream about them overseas."

He sat at the kitchen table which looked out across the large field at the rear of the barn. It ran all the way down to the southeastern shore of Lake Holly. His mother placed a large bake sheet of boulla rolls on the table beside him.

"I could fix an egg for you, son."

"No these boulla rolls will fill me up, Ma. By the way, Inger agreed to join me this morning for a swim in the lake. I've worked up a sweat already. Instead of taking a bath, I'll take a bar of soap down to the lake and lather up there. Dad told me that the rowboat engine still runs good, and there is a full tank of gasoline-enough to run around the lake a few times."

"It's nice to see you enjoying yourself, son. Inger has been good for you. There's a solidness to the girl that I like. Your father thinks so, too. Is it serious between you two, Joel?"

He knew she was going to ask the question. "Let me put it this way, Ma. We like each other enough to enjoy being together. Beyond that, I don't think I'm ready to make a commitment to a relationship that will end in marriage. I like Inger. I always have as you and Dad know, but the war has put a strain on everybody's lives. Once it's over, then we can start thinking of a future we can commit to. I talked a lot with the other wounded men in the hospital about a bill passed by congress giving veterans the opportunity to get a college education."

"Have you given any thought as to what you might want to do after the war? Your father said that a large project has been approved to build a four lane road from Kittery to Portland after the war. He could get you a job with his construction company," his mother mentioned.

He had heard rumors about the proposed roadway. It was a portion of a nationwide effort to connect most of the large cities with modern paved roads. "I'm not sure what I want to do, Ma. My main responsibility right now is to prepare myself for the welfare of the men in my command. Sometimes I worry that I'm not capable of the responsibility. Most of them are mere boys fresh out of high school. After their baptism of combat, they quickly become men, yet they look to me to make the decisions to carry out those missions assigned to us. I find that responsibility a heavy load, Ma."

His mother grasped her arms around his shoulders and kissed him on the head. "When we heard that you were promoted, our first thoughts were that you would handle the responsibility well. You're a lot like your father. He came home from the war a different man. When I first saw how his eyes seemed to look through a person into empty space, I was frightened. To this day, he has never talked about what he saw over there in France."

"I understand him better now, Ma. I also saw the penetrating stare, more so when I was a little boy," Joel told her, remembering those quiet moments with his father. "I hear footsteps on the porch. I bet it's Inger."

A knock on the front screen door announced Inger. "Hello, is anyone home?"

"Come in, Inger," Mrs. Thorn called. "There's some coffee left and a few more boulla rolls. Would you like some?"

Inger took a place at the table beside Joel and gently clasped his arm. "That would be nice, Mrs. Thorn. How are you doing now that you're home?" she asked Joel. She thought his color was better, and that pleased her.

"Home is what I needed. Ma is spoiling me rotten, and I love it," he grinned.

41

Mrs. Thorn served Inger a cup of coffee and a couple of rolls. "You might as well eat them while you can. They don't last long around the family."

"Thank you. It's a beautiful day out there," she exclaimed, sipping her coffee. "It's a good day to take a dip in the lake. I haven't been swimming this year yet."

Joel excused himself to put on a bathing suit under his pants. Then he and Inger checked the rowboat in the boathouse on the shore of the lake. The small Mercury engine was filled with gas as his mother had told him. Two pulls on the cord was all it took for the engine to spring to life. They shut it down and walked the boat out onto the lake and tied it to the dock.

"The water is warm," Joel declared, using a wash cloth and a bar of Lifeboy soap to lather his sweaty body. "I'm going to take a bath in the lake, and then we can go for a ride."

Inger removed her blouse and skirt and sat to unlace her shoes. She was a little shy and modest in her bathing suit. "The last one in is a rotten egg," she cried, leaping off the end of the dock.

Joel had been swimming with her every year of their lives. This was the first time he saw her as the mature young lady she was. Her modesty was becoming to her, yet she had always shown a streak of bashfulness. "I'll follow you. The physical therapy people at the hospital told me that swimming was a good exercise for me. The wounds have healed now."

"The water is great," she cried, several feet from the dock.

He lathered up and dove into the water to rinse the soap off, leaving a circle of soapy water behind him. There was a section of the lake just off the end of the dock that had several strong spring holes. The water pouring from the holes was a lot colder than the rest of the lake. "Wow, I had forgotten how cold those gushers of spring water could be," Joel smiled, swimming out to Inger.

She had a rubber bathing cap on to keep her hair from getting wet. "It's so nice to see you enjoying yourself, Joel. Would you like to check out Candy Island up on the northwest corner of the lake?"

"Sure," he replied. "I haven't been up there since Jimmy Sidlinger fell through the ice and drowned while we were fishing for lake salmon. That seems a long time ago. We were in the fifth grade then with Mrs. Pennington as our teacher."

Lake Holly was a relatively small lake of about two square miles. It was fed by springs with a runoff through the village where the water level was controlled by large removable planks in a dam near the center of town. The water quality was excellent with many households using the lake as a source of drinking water.

Joel and Inger cruised around the northern shore of the lake past a prominent peninsula known as Indian Point. They continued north where they saw several bob houses on the shore ready to be pulled back on the ice in the winter time when the ice was thick enough to hold their weight. The small shanties brought back a lot of memories for Joel. His father and friends looked forward

43

to hauling their bob house over some good fishing locations through the ice.

The house had a small stove that heated the interior and felt good when the wind swept across the lake with a fury. Two seats were constructed on each side of the house leaving room in the center for the men to chop a hole in the ice. The men could sit across from each other drinking coffee or tea with their fish lines in the water in relative comfort. The sport cultivated long lasting friendships. Joel recalled how good the food used to taste in the confined space of the house. The small stove opposite the door burned up dry firewood with a ferocious appetite. He had helped to haul firewood across the lake on his sled. He was always rewarded with a cup of cocoa with a dollop of marshmallow fluff and a warm boulla roll. Those were good times, and he smiled whenever he thought about them.

Joel maneuvered the boat to a small sandy shore on Candy Island and shut the engine down. He helped Inger out of the boat. She had brought a picnic basket with her containing ham sandwiches, boulla rolls and a thermos of coffee. The townspeople had built a picnic table and a small brick fireplace for their use. Occasionally, some people stayed all night on the small island. It was a peaceful spot with a view of the town and the steep hill south of the village. To the east and west mountains flanked the shore like sentinels standing guard.

"It's a pleasant location," Joel said, sitting at the wooden picnic table admiring the view. "I thought a lot about this place over the past few years. Sometimes I was afraid I'd never see it again. Did I ever tell you that when

I was a small boy I always wanted to check to see if there was any candy on the island. I had a big appetite for candy," he laughed.

Inger sat beside him laying her head against his shoulder. "I'm glad you came home. It has given you a chance to renew old memories and to find comfort in them. I've got to return to school tomorrow. New classes will start up. I'll be able to get my teaching certificate when this term ends in mid-winter. I'll be glad to have it over with."

"How does an old friend say thank you to a dear friend who is very generous and helpful?" Joel asked, placing an arm around her. "I'll miss you, Inger. These past few days have been important to me. I really appreciate your being a part of my homecoming."

"It has been a meaningful discovery for me, too, Joel. If I had the power to steal you away so that you did not have to return to active duty, I'd do it. But reality is always a sobering fact. You'll always be in my prayers and thoughts."

He kissed her and wiped the tears from her eyes. "I'm a lucky soldier. Remembering the good times helps to bring sanity to a soldier's life. Thanks for the memories. I heard Bob Hope repeat those lines several times in USO shows. It reminded me of you, Inger."

She softly wept in his arms there on Candy Island where her beloved was safe from harm. In a short time, that would change, and she was frightened for the future...

Chapter Six

Joel's good-bye to Inger was packed with emotion. Neither of them liked long drawn out scenes and were determined to make the parting brief. In each of their hearts, there was a sobering thought that they may never see each other again. Therefore, it was important for her to recall their last moments together.

"Come back to us, Joel," she said, clasping her arms around his neck. "I'll always be with you in spirit. Until next time, I love you. Good-bye…"

The past few days with Inger had given him peace of mind and contentment that had overpowered the trauma of the battlefields. He felt her warm lips and held her close to his heart. "I'll miss you, Inger. Thanks for the support. I wish you luck in school. I'll write as soon as I'm assigned to a regiment. Good-bye…"

She quickly released him and rushed to the taxi waiting to take her to the Boston and Maine train station.

That same day, Joel drove his Studebaker coupe to Jake Higgins, the only garage in town. He was still curious about the incident at the lookout and wanted to pick Jake's brain, hoping to get some clue as to the identity of the person. He was a middle-aged man just over the legal draft age with two children. His garage business provided a living for his family. Jake had a good reputation and was known for his competence.

"Hello, Jake," Joel announced himself inside the garage where Jake was greasing a Hudson Terraplane on the lift. "I was hoping you could give me a grease job and oil change on the Stude."

"It's nice to see you, Joel. We've been worried for you. Your dad has kept us informed. Sure, I can service your coupe just as soon as I finish this Hudson. I heard what happened to you up at the lookout."

"That's one of the things I wanted to speak to you about," Joel told him. "I've been curious about the woman. She was a total stranger to me."

"I had never seen her before either, Joel. She came to me just as I was closing the shop for the night. She was in a very nervous and impatient state of mind. I went up to pull her car out of the drainage ditch with my service truck. She paid me and left in a rush driving rapidly down the mountain."

"I remember the car was a Ford," Joel recalled.

"Yes, it was a 1941 Ford four-door sedan, pea green in color. The passenger side front fender had been damaged by a granite rock jutting from the bank of the ditch. I haven't seen her or the car since. I'm not sure if I'd even recognize her; it was too dark to see her features clearly."

Jake completed the Hudson and asked Joel to drive his coupe onto the lift ramp. Jake was very methodical, checking the tire pressure, exhaust system, and front end ball joints as he greased every fitting on the vehicle.

"I wish that I had gotten the registration number of the Ford. I remember she got into the car to start it while I hooked up a tow line," Jake mused. "The more I think about it, the more I recall that the plate looked in the darkness like a New Hampshire plate. I couldn't swear to it, Joel. I wish I could help you more. I told the deputy sheriff the same thing."

"I appreciate it, Jake. You did the best you could under the circumstances," Joel replied, putting the incident aside. "What are my chances of getting a set of tires for the Stude?"

"There aren't any new ones to buy. Your best chance is to get some used ones at a junk yard. Your tires are okay for a little longer. I could send them out to be recapped. It would take about two weeks to get them back."

"That sounds like a good idea. After I return to duty, Pa can drop the car off for you. I like the car very much. It's quite economical, too."

"Studebakers are good vehicles," Joel replied. "The Champ engine you have is the same as the one in my service truck. Studebaker Army trucks have earned a great reputation. We are sending thousands of them to Russia where they get brutal treatment."

Joel left Jake's garage thinking about the mystery lady. There was nothing new, and his pragmatism was strong enough to dismiss the issue until he had more time and information to pursue the matter further.

The next day he received orders to report to the Boston Hospital within the next forty-eight hours for a physical and additional orders for his next duty station.

The day before he left, Joel and his father stored his Studebaker coupe in the barn and removed the battery, placing it in a warm location in the cellar so that it would not freeze. It got cold in northern Maine in the wintertime.

Dressed in his best tan uniform, Joel said good-bye to the family and friends. His father drove him to the railroad station. Joel gave his father a bear hug, picked up his heavy duffel bag and quickly boarded the train. His father stood motionless, watching the train pull out of the station with a lump in his throat and tears straining for release. His heart ached, praying that this was not the last image he would have of his son.

Joel took a seat on the right side of the train known as the "Northeast Special" that ran from Belfast to Boston on a daily basis. For several miles he recognized the landscape and homes of old friends and associates in town. After a brief stop in Portland, the train ran down the Maine coast through Kennebunk, Wells and North Berwick before it crossed into New Hampshire at Dover. He had taken this same train ride when he joined the Army four years earlier. The train made a stop at Durham, New Hampshire, site of the University of New Hampshire campus. He casually looked at the line of automobiles parked at the large parking lot near the station when a 1941 light green four-door Ford sedan caught his eye.

Joel leaped from his seat to ask the conductor if he had time to get off for a moment to check out the automobile. He assured him that the train would be a few minutes loading milk from the University dairy farms. Joel ran to the vehicle to check the right hand fender. He found that it had a deep gash in the upper portion of the fender as if a rock or other sharp object had creased it. Now adrenaline was pumping through his body! He took out the small note pad he always carried in his vest pocket to copy down the license plate number.

"You better hurry, Captain," the conductor called to him.

Joel rushed back to the train excited that he probably had found a link to the identity of the mystery lady on the lookout rock. It could be a coincidence, but his gut reaction told him it was something tangible that could lead to a name and a person who was desperate enough to end her life! He took his notepad and printed: 1941 Ford light green four door sedan, License Plate No. NH937-207, located at parking lot of the University of New Hampshire campus.

The doctors at Boston were thorough in their examination of Joel and were satisfied that his recovery period was at an end. His release from the hospital contained the following statement: "Captain Joel Thorn is physically capable of carrying out any mission assigned to him. Official travel orders are enclosed." He was instructed to proceed by train to Fort Benning, Georgia, for instructions and training for a position in an infantry parachute regiment being formed for duty in the Pacific area.

He immediately called home to tell his mother who answered the phone about the vehicle he found in Durham. He gave her the number of the plate and asked her to check with the Deputy Sheriff in town if he could obtain the name and address of the owner.

"We'll do that, Joel. What a strange coincidence that you should locate such a vehicle," his mother replied.

"It might not be the same person, but it's worth a try, Ma," he replied, noting the long line of soldiers waiting to use the phone. "I've got to go, Ma. Give my love to everybody. I love you."

"We all love you too, son. What do we do if we find out who owns the car?"

"Well, you can tell me when I come home again. Right now I'm filled with expectations for my new duty station. "I'll fill you in when I get my new address. Good-by, Ma."

"Good-bye, son."

The train he took to Georgia was packed to capacity with soldiers and other servicemen and women. He thought it was strange that he was selected for duty with an air assault team. He was well trained and experienced with infantry tactics. The parachute was simply a means of inserting the soldier into the battlefield. He recalled that in Italy, near Anzio, his battalion had been the first to make contact with a parachute battalion that had jumped behind the lines to secure several bridges and to block the German's ability to reinforce and supply their line troops. They were a crack unit. His men had admired their discipline and tenacity under fire.

The parachute course was about four weeks long, depending on the infantry training experience of the men. He learned that there were several training facilities at Fort Bragg, N.C., and Fort Dix, N.J. The classroom

51

work for the few officers entered into the course was demanding and thorough, upholding the tradition of excellence that defined Benning. It was a complete review of infantry tactics as spelled out in the Army training manuals. The only exception was that the parachute battalions did not have the benefit of motorized supply units, kitchen facilities, or supporting arms available on demand. The parachute troops were traditionally known as "light infantry" capable of carrying out deep penetrations behind enemy lines. They were capable of very short engagements with the enemy unless they could receive additional supply from air drops or relief from ground troops. They were elite troops with a proud record of courage and audacity. Paratroopers had already established a tradition of excellence. The men were a proud, cocky outfit that expended more ammunition than any traditional battalion in the same situation and were assigned to more dangerous missions.

The training grounds at Lawson Airfield at the Benning Reservation was alive with activity. The only drawback to the brutal training schedule was the heat and the vast number of sand fleas and flies that penetrated their dungaree uniforms with ease. Several soldiers passed out from heat exhaustion. Joel was told that they were specifically selected to train in southern locations so as to acclimate them as much as possible for the tropical climate they would soon be fighting in. The daily routine was packed with body conditioning exercises, long walks in the dense southern forests, and intense emphasis on marksmanship at the rifle ranges.

The paratrooper was frequently alone to face a deadly enemy, and his skill as a rifleman was all he had to defend himself.

In between double-time physical activities, they were introduced to controlled jumps from 250-foot towers. They helped to lessen the natural fear of falling that every human being inherits from birth. The towers also increased their confidence and their ability to overcome difficult situations. Joel actually enjoyed the sensation of a controlled jump from the towers. He found that it gave him a euphoric sense of peace there on the training field.

Once he graduated to actual drops from an aircraft, he worried about the competence of the person who had packed his chute, but once that fear was overcome, he found the "silence" on the way to the ground soothing and exhilarating. He soon became a qualified parachutist assigned to the 315th Airborne Infantry Regiment. As pleased as he was with his assignment, he could not share it with his family or Inger.

Joel gave his new training assignment his best effort. The tempo of activity left him breathless. The Army was working at a rapid pace to produce units trained for combat in two theaters of war. Each morning began with classroom instruction of infantry tactics for battalions and regiments for several hours. The balance of the day was spent in the field working with the Benning training companies. They assaulted hilltops and heavily defended positions in all types of terrain as they planned each operation and implemented it.

Joel acted as commander of a reinforced battalion ordered to attack and destroy enemy forces at a prison compound several miles in a densely forested area. The assault had to be planned and executed in such a manner that the American inmates could be liberated before the enemy massacred them. He had no doubt that similar exercises would be performed once American forces returned to the Philippines. At the conclusion of each exercise, the officers got together to discuss their performance and to make suggestions for improvement.

Physical exercises continued every day. Joel lost ten pounds halfway through the training period. Then he slowly regained the same weight when body fat was turned into muscle. He was in the best physical condition he ever thought possible, and it gave him the confidence to perform any task assigned to his unit. Before he left Benning, he had several uniforms tailor-made so that they better fit his conditioned body. All of his classmates joked about how the Benning Infantry School was living up to its reputation for excellence.

The day Joel stood on the parade field with the graduating class passing in review was a proud moment for him. He had received a promotion to major assigned to the 315th Airborne Infantry Regiment as executive officer. The paratroop wings on his left chest just below his Combat Infantryman Badge made him proud. He was officially part of the Army's elite force. That night he wrote a letter home.

September 10, 1944

Dear Ma and Pa,

A few words tonight to inform you that I've been promoted to a major. With that rank I'm executive officer of a regiment. That position is usually given to a lieutenant colonel, but I've trained with the regiment and feel comfortable with the responsibility that comes with the new rank. The new pay scale will come in handy. I'm a happy man that my superiors had enough faith in my ability to fill the position even though I have never gone to college.

I plan to write Inger tonight also. Her letters have been coming regularly and make my day. Letters from home are the most effective morale booster in this man's Army.

My address will remain the same because I'm still with the same unit we trained with. Now we are on our way to a staging destination where we'll draw supplies and equipment prior to being shipped overseas. I always knew that we were destined for the Pacific area. That's all I can tell you for now.

Thanks for the letters and packages of chocolate chip cookies. They are a hit with everybody. Give my love to Sally. I've received a few letters from Maureen and have written to her. I'm proud of her desire to serve.

Goodnight. I love you both very much. Thanks for the support and the prayers. How fortunate I am to have you two for parents.

Love,

Joel

Chapter Seven

Shortly after completion of training at Benning, Joel was on a large troopship carrying his regiment to a staging island north of New Guinea with a large airfield. It had recently been captured by MacArthur's forces as one of the stepping stones toward the Philippines. He was determined to keep his promise to the Filipino people to return. Now he had the forces sufficient to accomplish that goal. Joel's regiment had been prepared for duty in the tropics with multiple inoculations to prevent endemic tropical diseases and they had been taking atabrine tablets to prevent malaria ever since they left San Francisco. They already had that bronze complexion the tablets produce on the skin.

The regiment was double-timed off the ship to the docks covered with mountains of supplies and vehicles of every type in the Army's arsenal parked in symmetrical lines. A large airfield was located adjacent to the supply depot. The bivouac for the regiment was on the opposite side of the airfield, so the regiment marched two miles with full packs to the tented area.

Joel and the regiment's officers were instantly called for a conference at a newly constructed Quonset metal building next to the tent area. He knew it was an important conference when a skeptical looking sergeant guarding the entrance stated: "You are warned, Major Thorn, that what you see or hear here, stays here. Is that clear?"

"It is, Sergeant," Joel replied, returning his salute.

The conference room was set up with tables in a circle so that everyone present could see each other. Joel recognized General Walter Krueger, commander of the Eighth Army, standing with his back to the conference table studying a map. He turned to greet the officers when one of his staff called the meeting to order. There was a nervous silence in the room as General Krueger threw his hat on the table and walked to the map with a pointer in his hand.

"Gentlemen," he began in a clear voice with a slight accent. "We are about to engage the Japanese on the smaller islands in Leyte Gulf on our way to a complete liberation of the Philippine Archipelago. You will be part of an historical campaign to destroy the Japanese armies that have become embedded in the islands. Now to be more specific," he said, pointing to a small dot in Leyte Gulf on the map, "here is our first objective of a powerful drive to free the Filipino people. This is an island in the Gulf protecting the approaches to the larger island of Leyte. Are the officers of the 315th Infantry Parachute Regiment present?"

Joel stood up and said, "I'm Major Thorn, executive officer of the regiment. Our commanding officer, Colonel Haynes, was seriously injured on board our transport and was unable to attend this conference. I'm acting temporarily as commanding officer. The battalion officers are all present, General."

"Are you prepared to lead the full regiment in an air drop on the enemy, Major?" General Kruger casually requested.

"The ship's doctor told me that Colonel Haynes would not be able to walk for a few weeks. I'm senior officer in the regiment," Joel told him.

"Do you want me to assign a Colonel to your regiment?" General Kruger pointedly asked.

"You may do so if you think it's appropriate, General. I've trained with the regiment, and I'd consider it a privilege to lead the men in their first engagement with the enemy if you approve, Sir."

Joel's answer was what the General wanted to hear. He smiled, and nodded his head, "You've got your chance, Major Thorn. Your regiment has been selected to secure an airfield and a bridge on this small island in the Gulf of Leyte. You will have the distinction of leading your regiment in its first offensive and our first operation against the Japanese in the Philippine Islands."

"We are ready, Sir!"

The chronology of events leading up to and including the air assault by the 315th were discussed in general terms at the conference. Specific orders and timetables would be spelled out in detail in orders to the various units involved. The conference was over, and Joel, excited about the coming operation, saw to it that his regiment was being taken care of and food made available to them. That night they occupied the temporary tents for a good night's sleep. The next day they were scheduled to receive additional supplies, weapons, and ammunition for the proposed assault. Eighth Army operations office told Joel to expect orders at any moment and to be prepared to load men and equipment aboard several DC-3 aircraft on the airfield at least an hour prior to sunrise.

That night, Joel sat quietly in his tent writing letters. The fact that he would be in combat within twenty-four hours did not bother him as much as it had when he was inexperienced in North Africa. The young officers had looked up to him for advice and council ever since they started their training at Benning. He held their trust as a sacred commitment to try harder.

Somewhere in the Pacific

October 4, 1944

Dear Inger,

A few words tonight on the eve of combat to tell you that I received four of your letters all at once today. They are a wonderful source of strength and hope to me. I cannot tell you where I am. How nice it is to have a link back to our small world at Lake Holly.

It's nice to know that you have an offer to teach the fourth grade in town. I remember our fourth grade teacher, Miss Earl. I can honestly tell you that I had a crush on her. Don't laugh, I really did...

I'm proud of you, Inger, and am looking forward to that time when the war is over and we can get our lives back on track.

Tonight, I've officially taken control of the regiment even though I'm just a major. Normally it is given to a full colonel. I only hope that I'm up to the task. The men are terrific, but oh so young and

59

innocent. Some of them will be lost and never return home to their loved ones after our first mission. That fact weighs heavily on my mind. I pray that I'm capable of the responsibility handed to me.

Pray for us, Inger. These brave young boys are about to be turned into men and seasoned combat soldiers. That is a cruel reality I wish could be by-passed, but we'll handle it like the soldiers we are.

Thanks for being there for me. Your support sustains me every day.

All my love,

Joel

D-Day came the next morning. DC-3 transports were waiting for them on the runway. Two Battalions of the regiment were to jump on the operational area of the Japanese airfield on the target island. The area contained the most heavily fortified defenses along with barracks and operational facilities. The third battalion was given the task of dropping to secure a bridge over a waterway connecting two islands capable of being turned into a larger airfield and staging area for the assaults being planned for the Philippines. The capture and holding of the bridge was estimated to be the easier task of the operation. Intelligence gave no indication of any concentrations of enemy soldiers.

Support for Joel's regiment was known as Operation Rolling Thunder, and support was available from Naval aircraft stationed on a carrier in Leyte Gulf. Stubby Navy Hellcats fighter planes had already softened up the operational area of the airfield. It was hoped that the regiment could capture the airfield intact for immediate use by Army Air Corps aircraft.

Joel planned to stay with the two battalions that landed on the airstrip. Intelligence had a way of being wrong, and he was concerned about isolating the men in third battalion. He urged the battalion commander to keep in radio contact with him at all times for progress reports. Joel told him that Navy air support was only a few minutes away for either of them. That gave them a more secure feeling, but that little voice in Joel's consciousness made him uneasy.

The paratroops planned to jump at dawn so that the sun out of the east would temporarily blind the enemy as they were floating to the ground. Joel led his command by example and was the first to jump out of the lead transport plane. Soon, the sky was filled with white chutes gently dropping to the ground. Joel was carrying his normal limit of ammunition and hand grenades with a .45 pistol on his belt and a Thompson sub-machine gun with two clips, holding twenty-five bullets each, taped together for a quick change. A service knife was in a sheath in his boot.

As soon as his chute opened, he turned the safety on his Thompson. The gun was now ready to fire. He searched the ground for activity. Several fortified machine gun emplacements were already shooting at his men. They had intentionally made a short drop of about 800 feet so that their vulnerability to ground fire was cut to a minimum. That was little consolation to Joel who saw several chutes with men hanging loosely from the shrouds. Their loss ignited a raging fury within his breast. He had trained and lived with these men admiring the dedication and commitment that motivated them.

Once he hit the ground, he threw two grenades towards a gun pit close by. Immediately after the explosion, he sprayed the area with his Thompson and quickly shed his chute. He jumped into the machine gun nest behind sand bags, screaming for his radioman. To those men within his voice range he ordered to form a strike force to neutralize the operations building. They advanced behind exploding grenades towards the building. One grenade took out the entrance door. They carefully entered the wooden structure systematically clearing every room with grenades before entering. Shortly, Joel declared the building secured. No prisoners were taken. The Japanese were different than the Germans who would surrender when their situation looked hopeless.

Joel left the building to survey the situation. It appeared as if the operational area had the least number of troops. He called the Army command post. "Rolling Thunder to Command, Operations building beside the airport is secured. Small pockets of resistance are being wiped out..."

As he was speaking, a massive explosion threw rocks and gravel into the air all across the runway, rendering the airfield temporarily unusable. A ditch two feet deep ran the full width of the runway. Joel explained what had just taken place and suggested that bulldozers be routed first onto the island for repair of the runway.

An urgent SOS sounded on the radio from third battalion. "Major Thorn, this is Captain Haynes. Large numbers of Japanese troops are coming from the hills west of the airfield. Urgent, we need assistance. We may not be able to hold our position on the bridge, out."

"Haynes, this is Major Thorn. I'll see what I can do. We have no vehicles, but I'll organize a flying column to relieve you. Ration your ammo and call the Navy for support. We'll get there as soon as we can. Good luck, Captain."

Joel instantly called for two platoons from his original company to replenish their ammo and grenade supply from canisters dropped with the troops. He told them to shed any excess weight so that they could rush to the aid of their friends in third battalion. He called the command post to inform them of his decision to reinforce the bridge detachment, and that their estimate of numbers of Japanese soldiers was wildly incorrect and had placed them in jeopardy.

The flying column left the airport center at a fast jog with Joel setting the pace. Halfway there they saw enemy troops flowing from the hillside to the west. Joel was concerned for the third battalion. The area was swarming with the enemy! He called for his radioman to come beside him so that he could call in support in case Captain Haynes had not done so.

"Rolling Thunder calling Navy Fire Control. We are desperately in need of assistance."

"Rolling Thunder, this is Navy Fire Control. I'm switching you to Blue Boy One who is now airborne on his way to render assistance. We suggest that you use the aircraft for the time being. We do not fire the ship's guns when friendly aircraft is in the vicinity. They have potent capabilities to handle whatever you need done. Good luck paratroopers, out."

"Blue Boy to Rolling Thunder. We are on our way to assist you. Third battalion has informed us of his situation and that you are enroute to assist his force at the bridge. Third battalion will outline their perimeter with smoke or phosphorous grenades, so that we do not violate their security."

"This is Rolling Thunder to Blue Boy. Situation understood. Continue your contact with Captain Haynes of third battalion, out."

Joel's relief column had another mile to reach the bridge when small arms fire erupted from the open area between the airfield and their line of travel. He hollered for the men to pull their weapons off safety and to continue the pace to third battalion. As they drew closer to the bridge, he was concerned about the integrity of their column. Enemy opposition was increasing. Several Japanese soldiers charged out of the jungle with fixed bayonets to halt their progress.

"Don't stop, men. Defend yourself, but don't stop," Joel hollered, emptying his twenty-five round magazine at the formation of Japanese soldiers. Before he could replace the clip a soldier leaped in front of him intent on using his bayonet. Joel was quick enough to parry the bayonet. Joel dropped his Thompson letting it hang on his shoulder and drew the knife from the sheaf on his right leg. He closed with the Japanese soldier and drove the knife three times into his stomach and side. A look of fear filled the enemy's eyes as Joel removed the blade and continued on his way.

At that moment, three Navy Hellcats came over the column at a low altitude and turned towards the mountainous region to their left firing rockets into a mass of enemy soldiers running towards the bridge. They continued to fire their machine guns into enemy formations and turned to strafe the area parallel to their column. A cheer pierced the lips of the paratroopers as they entered the defensive perimeter third battalion had placed around the valuable bridge.

The planes emptied their weapons and dropped three canisters of napalm (liquid gasoline) between the bridge and the mountains. However, the Japanese continued to threaten their defenses in ever increasing numbers. Joel and Captain Haynes were both afraid they would run out of ammunition. Joel called for assistance as the Hellcats left the area. "Navy Fire Control, this is Thunder One. We are in danger of being overrun we have a limited amount of ammunition left."

"Thunder One, this is Navy Fire Control. Now that the Hellcats have left the area we can provide support from a cruiser with twelve-inch turret guns. It is now under way, please stay on the line to monitor our range and accuracy."

Seconds later, an explosion landed 500 feet north of their location. Joel called back: "Navy Fire Control, you are right on target. Fire at will, walking your shots northward and slightly easterly. That hillside is the source of our trouble, out."

The entire hillside erupted in smoke and rubble. The twelve inch shells devastated several miles of jungle turning it into a smoldering waste land. "My God," Joel exclaimed, turning to his radio man. "Call Navy Fire Control and thank them for the thorough job of eliminating any nearby opposition to our control of the bridge."

A few minutes after the naval bombardment ceased, a call came from Blue Boy One that they were on their way to give support until ground troops relieved them. He also asked them to define their perimeter with smoke or phosphorous grenades.

"Thunder One, this is Blue Boy One. We see your perimeter. We will patrol in a five mile circle until you are relieved. If you need support, just call. Good Luck, Army."

The paratroopers felt secure beneath the dark blue Navy Hellcats. They waited patiently, scanning the rubble around them for any movement of Japanese troops. An hour later, they were relieved of the responsibility for the integrity of the bridge by several LVT amphibian tractors filled with infantry.

Joel called Army Command and told them that Operation Rolling Thunder was successfully concluded.

"Army Command to Rolling Thunder. A hearty 'well done' to you and your men, Major. You've shortened our timetable to Leyte. Report to Island Command as soon as you've been relieved and had a hot meal."

Chapter Eight

Joel ordered a conference for all officers of the 315th regiment in a large mess tent beside the airfield they had secured. The small island quickly became an active staging and supply area for advances through the Philippines. They had just experienced their baptism of fire, and Joel was anxious to evaluate their performance.

They had absorbed relatively light casualties considering the numbers of Japanese on the island. They had twenty killed and 30 wounded in action. Every officer in the regiment except for Joel had the gut-wrenching task of notifying the men's families. Nothing in life prepares the officers for such a difficult duty. Joel still reflected on how he handled the men in search of some way he might have accomplished the mission with fewer casualties. The responsibility humbled him every day.

The burden of leading young men into the jaws of death was one every officer had to deal with. Frequently the units ordered into battle were at the mercy of erroneous intelligence reports such as they had experienced on this island. They could be disastrous, and a good officer on the ground had to deal with the reality. Nothing replaced good old fashioned common sense and

67

the discipline to listen to that little voice every officer carries with him into the crucible of war.

Joel had just completed a review of the regiment's performance over several cups of coffee when a colonel from Sixth Army asked for permission to intrude on their deliberations.

"You're welcome to our gathering, Colonel Prescott." Joel stood to salute the Colonel.

"You and your paratroopers did a great job, Major Thorn. I've come to ask a favor of you and your regiment." Colonel Prescott took a seat next to Joel and accepted a cup of hot coffee.

"How can we help you, Colonel?" Joel asked him.

"To be brief, we just received word from our partisan comrades on Leyte that the inmates in a small prison camp we had no previous knowledge of are in imminent danger of being massacred as soon as we launch an attack against the island. As you already know, we are in the process of conducting several rescue operations with the Ranger units in Sixth Army. They will secure and hold the POW camps that we know exist. This newest one is in southern Leyte. One of our Ranger battalions sent word to us about this camp. Some of their inmates had been detained at the unknown facility."

"Didn't this camp show up in your aerial photos?" Joel asked.

"The answer is no, Major. Once we had approximate coordinates we closely examined our photos. We then found that the camp was so artfully camouflaged that it did not show up as an obvious prison site."

"My head is filled with questions. Why don't you tell us what you want us to do? If there are prisoners in danger of being massacred, I speak for the regiment when I say we are available to assist them," Joel exclaimed.

Colonel Prescott was visibly relieved. "My reason for coming is to ask you to select forty to sixty men to secure the compound and hold it until our ground troops invade the island. You have my word that as soon as that takes place a flying column will be sent to you with all the ability to reinforce your strength and to transport the prisoners to safety and medical care. That's a promise, Major. We're scheduled to assault the southern portion of Leyte in thirty-six hours. Time is precious, Major."

"Are you considering an air drop or a penetration behind enemy lines?" Joel inquired.

"An air drop would trigger the retaliation we are afraid of, Major. We can insert you on the island by submarine or PT boat under the cover of darkness. The camp is about five miles from the western coast. We have partisans that are prepared to guide you through the jungle to the camp."

"Why can't they capture it, Sir?"

"They do not have enough manpower or radio communications to guide air support and the relief column to assist you. All of the Filipino guerilla units have been alerted to assist our efforts. A few camps have already been liberated," Colonel Prescott was pleased to announce.

"I understand, Sir. I did not mean to imply that they should do the job," Joel turned to the Colonel. "I can have two platoons ready to leave in an hour, Colonel. I'll lead them on the mission with one request, Sir. Would it be possible for you to incorporate the remaining men in the regiment into the relief column?"

The Colonel smiled and stood up. "You must have read my mind, Major. I will personally insert your regiment into the vanguard of the assault units. We will have air support available for you as well as Naval gunfire support which can reach the location of the compound. Naval gunnery is potent and reasonably accurate considering the platform they're firing from."

"Can you fit two platoons on a PT boat, Colonel?"

"Probably not, but we do have available several Army patrol vessels with shallow draft manned by the Coast Guard. They are an efficient team that have impressed us with their competence and 'can do' attitude. As soon as you secure the compound, we will have planes available to drop food, medicine, and clothing for the inmates. General MacArthur is passionate about letting the people of the Philippines know that we have not forgotten them. Therefore, rescue missions have top priority of resources."

"We share your concern and are proud to be a part of the rescue effort, Colonel Prescott."

"Thanks for the support, Major. I'll get the ball rolling. You can expect to be picked up by eleven PM at the landing site. Engineers have already built a dock to offload supplies. We can use the same code name for this endeavor, Major. Rolling Thunder seems appropriate for your paratroopers. I'll see to it that ammo and c-rations are available at the loading dock. Good luck."

Joel turned to the men at the table. "There it is, you heard the man. Any comments?"

Captain Holmes raised his hand and said, "I want to volunteer two platoons from my company, Major, and I'd consider it a privilege to accompany you on this mission."

Joel knew that Captain Holmes was a graduate of Virginia Military Institute with much combat experience. He was older than Joel and had a reputation of being outspoken to superior officers who assumed a superior air of authority within the ranks. The men idolized him for his passionate concern for their welfare. Joel liked him for his honesty and straight talk. He was the kind of man one could depend on in a crunch. "Captain Holmes, I'll be glad to have you with us. Your two platoons will prepare themselves for the mission. The rest of you can enjoy a good night's sleep. We'll meet you in a couple of days at the prison compound. God bless all of you."

It was a beautiful night in the tropics. The moon was full with not a cloud in the sky — perfect for a clandestine walk in the jungle. Joel and Captain Holmes had the men assemble at the waterfront where they filled their packs to capacity with ammunition and c-rations. Everybody used a Thompson sub-machine. It was a deadly weapon for close-in fighting and had a reputation of being reliable in all kinds of weather. At about nine-thirty the men were resting on the sand when a patrol boat tied up to the dock.

A Chief Petty Officer jumped to the dock and walked to the group of soldiers. "Which one of you is Major Thorn?"

"I'm Major Thorn," Joel replied.

"I'm Chief Petty Officer Meyers of the Coast Guard. I've been ordered to insert you and your men at a point on the western side of Leyte. We have a converted Army supply boat with a shallow draft. I've been told you will have about fifty men. It will be a little crowded, but we'll make do."

"Our revised number is forty men, Chief. They are the best of the best," Joel told him.

"Welcome aboard, soldiers. Make yourself comfortable on the rear deck or in the cabin. I prefer not to have anyone in front of the pilot's shelter."

"Okay, men," Joel directed. "Weapons on safety, and magazines detached. Double check that there is no cartridge in the chamber. Rest the best you can. It might be wise to take a little nourishment from one of your C-Rations. It looks as if we'll be busy for the next twenty-four hours."

Joel and Captain Holmes joined Chief Meyers in the pilot cockpit. The chief introduced the two soldiers to the helmsman. "This is Seaman Clark. He has carefully studied the charts of the area where we are going to deposit your soldiers. These Army patrol boats are manned by Coast Guardsman. There are hundreds of them in use in the Pacific area. This particular boat has on board a fathometer and a gyro compass which Clark monitors often. We can navigate close to shore where regular sea-going vessels would never be able to travel. We have a four-man detachment of Coasties on board with three twin mounts of fifty-caliber machine guns. Our Coast Guard command has placed navigational signals on a submerged barge in the Leyte Gulf. We constantly monitor that signal and can navigate accurately to any point along the Leyte coastline."

"I'm impressed with the professionalism of the Coast Guard, Chief," Joel told him. "How long do you estimate before we make contact with our guides?"

"We should be at the rendezvous by midnight, Major. We'll take you ashore in our inflatable rafts so that you or your equipment does not have to get wet."

"We appreciate that."

"I'm going to leave you and man the forward machine gun mount. For a small patrol boat we have a lot of firepower. Quite often PT boats chase barges into shallow water and call on us to finish them off. We've sunk over two dozen Japanese barges and landing crafts."

Joel smiled at the Chief. He was typical of the chiefs in the Navy and Coast Guard and the sergeants in the Army who really run the services. He and Captain Holmes found a vacant spot near the cockpit to sit down and relax until they reached their destination. Two hours later, the hum of the two Continental engines was idled down, and the patrol craft made a sharp turn to the starboard. Slowly the craft dodged rocks and came to a complete stop with engines closed down.

Chief Meyers kneeled down beside Joel. "We'll have three rafts in the water ready for you, Sir. We can take six men on each, so my men will make three trips to shore. We are only about fifty feet from the beach. Your guides are already there. They have signaled their presence as we approached."

Joel was in the lead raft to the beach. He had the first wave of three boats to take a defensive stance in a semi-circle inland as far as the vegetation. They were to wait there until all the men had come ashore. Joel watched the jungle for any sound or movement that he could detect in the full moonlight. Within minutes the Coasties had conveyed all of his contingent ashore.

Joel began to assemble the men in a line when a soft voice close by startled him: "You must be Rolling Thunder."

"Yes, we are Rolling Thunder," Joel answered, keeping his voice down. "I'm relieved to know that we've made contact with you. I'm Major Thorn. We have forty-two men for this mission."

"I'm Lieutenant Smart. How nice it is to hear American voices. I've been here on Leyte ever since the Japanese took over the islands."

"Are you alone, Lieutenant?"

"I have a squad of ten men surrounding our rendezvous to intercept any intruders into the area. We should start for the compound now. Your Coast Guard crew was confident they could get you here in the dark without a hitch. They've been bringing supplies to me for about a month now. The Coast Guard has made me proud to be an American," Lieutenant Smart said.

"I agree with you, Lieutenant. You must be anxious to be liberated. It won't be long now."

"At first we doubted that MacArthur would keep his word. Our first indication that he would keep his promise were little packets called 'victory boxes' dropped by planes on our hideout in the northern mountains. They were filled with candy, thread and needle, gum and cigarettes. On the exterior of the small carton were the words 'I shall return'. I'll never forget that moment of sheer joy. Morale went up 110 percent in our guerilla camp."

"You're a courageous soldier, Lieutenant. By the way, do I detect a New England twang in your voice?" asked Joel, guessing he was from New England.

"I'm a Swede from North Adams, Massachusetts, near the Vermont border. I served in the Army during the first war and decided to make it a career. I was promoted from sergeant to second lieutenant just before the Japs hit us at Pearl Harbor. General MacArthur promoted me to a first lieutenant early during the Japanese occupation. I could have left the islands on one of the submarines that supplied us over the years, but my men who escaped capture, and my dear Filipino friends needed me. I've never regretted the decision to stay and harass the Japanese every chance we could. As soon as the Americans kick the Japs out of the Leyte, I'm going back home, and I'm never going to leave."

"You certainly deserve it, Lieutenant. We have something in common. I'm a mustang also. I joined up in 1940 as a private."

"My men will secure our flanks as we walk to the compound. Caution your men that we should be as quiet as possible especially keeping metal canteens from banging about," Lieutenant Smart suggested. "It will take us about two hours to get to a meadow beside the camp. I'll describe the compound to you at that time when the light will be a little bit better, and you can observe the area. I took the liberty of refusing an air attack prior to our assault from the ground. It would trigger a massacre by the Japanese who survived the air attack."

"I agree with your reasoning," Joel answered in a low voice.

"When I show you the layout of the compound, Major, you can plan the tactic to secure it. My men will be alert on the outskirts to give warning if any Jap troops enter the area. I doubt if we encounter that, but we may once the invasion starts."

"I was concerned about that, Lieutenant. We are fortunate to have you as a guide."

The paratroopers were amazed at the noise that enveloped them once they entered the thick jungle. Creatures of the night filled the air with a cacophony of disjointed sounds foreign to most Americans. The heavy canopies overhead blocked most of the moonlight from entering the ground. The men followed close behind each other wondering in the darkness if a Jap soldier was lurking, waiting to kill the intruders. They carried their Thompsons loaded with safety off, ready to fire once the lever was released.

For two hours they walked in silence, keeping pace with Joel and Lieutenant Smart, walking through shallow mountain streams and over sharp rock formations. Smart placed a hand on Joel's shoulder, motioning for him to kneel on the ground. "I want to show you the sketch I have of the compound. Would your men hold this tarp on top of us so that no light can be seen? We are within two hundred yards of the compound. The men should rest and remain very quiet."

Joel had the men pass on the word and pulled the canvas over his head and shoulders. Lieutenant Smart laid out a large sketch of the compound and shone his flashlight on it. He pointed to a cluster of buildings with a ten foot fence around it, and to five guard stations positioned on elevated platforms evenly spaced around the camp. Joel knew that his first tactic was to neutralize the five guard posts at the same time.

"How many Japs are in the camp, Lieutenant?"

"We estimate approximately twenty to thirty at most. They are concentrated at the barracks building, their headquarters building at the northern end of the compound, and of course at each of the guard posts." He pointed to those facilities on the map. "Inside the wire fence are the open latrine pits, small thatched roof shelters where the inmates sleep, and about one hundred graves. The stench from the camp is overpowering."

"How many American soldiers are in the camp?" Joel inquired.

"There aren't any soldiers, Major. There are about fifty female inmates detained by the Japanese when they took over. Most are Americans with a few other nationalities!"

Chapter Nine

"Women POWs!" Joel exclaimed. "We were not told anything about the inmates. I just assumed they would be American soldiers. Now I understand the need for speed in securing the compound. In what condition are the prisoners? We may not be able to move them away from the camp."

Lieutenant Smart recalled the last time he was able to view the camp from a distance. "My personal opinion is that the inmates are as close to 'walking dead' as human beings can be. It's a pathetic sight, Major. They are gaunt and weary and probably are praying for death to take them from the cesspool they have been living in for years. Basic nutrition and medical care have long since passed them by. The size of the cemetery is an indication of what they have endured."

Joel was angered by Smart's description. "Your rough sketch tells me that we should break up into six assault teams of five to six men so that we hit the guard towers and the front gate all at the same time. I'm in favor of forming a solid ring of protection around the inmates once the towers and gate have been destroyed. It's important that we let the women know who we are and for them to lay down on the ground until we secure the compound."

"That sounds like a sound plan, Major. I can lead three of the teams around the perimeter to the east to neutralize those towers," Lieutenant Smart volunteered.

"Okay, Lieutenant. I hope to take charge of the other towers and the front gate quickly. Surrounding the inmates' shelters once the towers are blown is very important. That way we bring our entire force together to repel any attacks by the remainder of the security forces. We are bypassing the headquarters and barracks meaning we can expect an attempt to hit our protective ring around the inmates. Once we take out the gate and towers, those points are the only access to the inmates and our blocking stance. We'll have to evaluate that situation once we've joined forces. How long will it take to secure the towers, Lieutenant Smart?"

"About a half hour."

Joel checked his watch in the poor light. "Okay, men. You squad leaders organize the six teams. It's now 7:10. Synchronize your watches. At 7:45 on the second, we'll blow the five towers, the gate, and eliminate any Japanese that may be within the compound. That's important. In doing that, we can probably reduce the Japanese force by twenty percent. Join ranks quickly around the shelters. Any questions?"

There was movement as the men selected partners within the teams. A squad leader corporal spoke for the force. "Those bastards are going to find that they're up against the first team. Don't worry about us, Major."

Joel smiled. "Good luck men. Let's get Rolling Thunder in motion. Happy landings."

Six men joined with Joel to blow the front gate. They successfully crawled through the wet meadow to within a few feet of the gate. They were soaking wet, but it felt good after sweating in the humid air of the tropics with their heavy packs. Joel silently indicated for two of the men to act as rear guards against Japanese soldiers from the two structures close to the gate. The others, with Joel leading them, crawled even closer to the gate. He checked his watch. They had twenty seconds before zero hour! Four men with Joel in the lead, ran desperately for the gate with grenades ready. Four Japanese soldiers were caught unaware of their presence until the grenades exploded. They were blown up when the gate was pulverized. Echoes of explosions all around the perimeter erupted at the same time.

The shelters for the women inmates were open on all four sides. The thatch roof was the only protection they had from the elements. The teams were screaming that they were Americans and for the women to stay in their shelters. Sporadic gunfire could be heard on the eastern perimeter. The protective ring of forty paratroopers very effectively shrunk the area they had to fortify.

Joel entered the compound as soon as the gates went up in pieces. The shelters seemed to hold about six or seven people lying on bamboo mats on the ground. There was no furniture and no nets to protect them from mosquitoes and other insects prominent in the tropics. "Do not be afraid. We are American soldiers and have come to set you free. Do not be afraid. Please stay low on your mats. We are American soldiers," Joel called out to the inmates.

Two figures at the shelter closest to the gate dressed in ragged and tattered clothing rose from their bamboo mats to approach Joel with their skeleton-like arms reaching out to him. Sickened by the hollow, deep-set eyes, and legs and arms like small children, he was moved by their presence. He had never witnessed human beings so pitiful in his life. He slung the Thompson over his shoulder, and reached out for the two figures. "I'm Major Thorn. We are American soldiers, and have come to set you free. We have not yet secured the camp. Do you understand me?"

Both women had grotesque facial features with skin stretched tightly against protruding bone structures. He clasped their tiny hands in his. They were trying to tell him something. Their voices were low as if it was difficult for them to speak. They pointed to the headquarters building behind them in a beseeching manner. "We are Americans." One said and immediately began to sob, hiding her face in her filthy hands.

The older woman with white straggly hair looked Joel in the eye and said in a faint voice, "Our friends... The beasts have some of our friends in the building to satisfy their lust...They have been crying for help, and we cannot help them," she cried.

Her pleas for help touched Joel, igniting a rage that fueled his decision to assault the building. He screamed for his six-man team to follow him into the building and for the balance of the men to cover his vacant portion of the protective circle around the shelters. He approached

81

the front entrance of the building with a grenade rolling it against the door, quickly stepping to one side. The door went up in pieces. He leaped through the opening holding his Thompson off safety.

The hall was filled with Japanese soldiers. Several had been wounded by the splinters and explosion of the grenade. Joel assessed the situation and dropped another grenade in the hallway as he smashed into a door near the entrance. The explosion threw him into the room against a bed with a woman screaming. Her eyes were filled with fear. Two Japanese officers were in the room with drawn pistols. They too were shaken by the explosion. Joel's reflexes were quicker. He squeezed the trigger of his Thompson holding the nose down to concentrate on the enemy officers. They collapsed on the floor.

He heard shouts from his team hollering "all clear". Joel shouted, "all clear," and stepped into the hallway. It was cluttered with human body parts. They had been lucky to catch several enemy soldiers in one location where the grenades wreaked a vicious vengeance. There were four rooms in the headquarters building. They had been cleared of Japanese. His team reported to Joel that there were women in all four rooms. Some were still screaming and weeping.

Joel's instinct to help the women was delayed until they had secured the barracks. He was in the process of ordering the members of his team to hit the barracks when explosions erupted blowing several windows in the headquarters building. The barracks and everyone in the structure went up with a horrific explosion. None of his team had gone near the building. Joel was puzzled by the explosion and ran outside to see what was going on.

He met Lieutenant Smart. "What in hell was that all about, Lieutenant?"

"We never got near it, Major. I'll bet the remaining Jap soldiers touched off munitions in their own barracks. They never surrender. They'll take their own lives when all is lost. They saved us the trouble of sending them to the next world."

"I'll be damned," Joel exclaimed. "Lieutenant, would you take a couple of my men and reconnoiter the compound area to make sure we have eliminated all resistance? We've got to help these inmates. Pass the word, I want my radio man, on the double."

Joel waved for his team to empty the building and went into the room where he had shot two officers. They were no longer a threat. The two cots in the room each had a desperate crying woman. He slung his Thompson over his shoulder and kneeled beside the two cots to calm the women.

"Please, do not be afraid. I'm an American soldier and have come to set you free. They can't hurt you anymore. Please, do you understand me? I'm an American soldier..."

Both females stopped crying and opened their eyes to look at him. He had never in his life seen such pathetic looking human beings. Their deep-sunken eyes stared at him as if they were not seeing him clearly. Later, he would learn that all of the inmates were suffering from some degree of blindness caused by their starvation diet over the years. The two women used blankets to cover their nakedness. Tears filled their eyes. What could he say to such pitiful women? He felt totally helpless. He wanted to do something but what? He showed them the American flag on his left shoulder and repeated, "I'm an American soldier. The Japanese cannot hurt you anymore."

"Major Thorn," a voice called for him. It was Corporal Jameson, his radio man.

"I'm in the first room on the left, Jameson," Joel answered.

Jameson saw the two dead officers. "The other rooms have women in them. One has already died from fright I guess."

"These people need everything, Jameson. Get on the radio and call Command Center. Tell them what we have here. We need food, medical supplies, clothing, female sanitary supplies, and additional ammunition in case we have to hold off an attack. Tell them it's an emergency. These people are all on the precipice of death, and we must save them. Also inform them to start our relief column in motion with our regiment leading the way. Rolling Thunder insists on priority of effort. No one would believe what we've discovered here in this hellhole. I want action, not promises. Give it your best shot in my name, Jameson."

"Consider it done, Major," Jameson replied, leaving the building for better reception on his backpack radio.

The two women were quietly lying on the cots with blankets wrapped around them. They heard what had been said, and the reality of their situation had registered with both of them. It took a while for them to realize that they were truly free. Freedom was a phenomenon they had only dreamed about. A few hours before the Americans came, every woman in the compound had lost the will to live. Death was a path to release from all the misery and pain.

Captain Holmes called for Joel who left the building to confront Holmes. His report was given between gasps of breath. The area had a putrid, vile smell that clogged air passages. It was the smell of death. The protective circle around the shelters had been completed. Outposts had been stationed beyond the barbed wire fence to alert them of any approaching enemy.

"I've ordered supplies dropped, Harvey. Now we need to locate water and any foodstuff that the Japs may have had. They need nourishment and water to cleanse their bodies." Joel desperately told him.

"I just spoke to Lieutenant Smart. He was having a conference with his Filipino partisans. They've placed a wide security ring around this compound. If they detect enemy movements that are a threat to us, we'll be notified so we can deflect an attack. He's a hell of a good man. I'll check on Japanese supplies," Captain Holmes informed Joel and left.

Several women wrapped in blankets came out of the building. One approached Joel with a determined look that caught Joel's attention. "What can I do for you, Ma'am?"

The woman answered in halting phrases and a very weak voice: "I was with the women in the officer's building..." she cried out to him. Her dark hair was streaked with white flags, horribly soiled and snarled.

Her hands grasping the blanket to her body were nothing but bones with stretched skin covering them. They were like a small child.

"I'm Major Thorn. I've sent for supplies to be delivered. Where did the Japanese guards eat?"

She pointed to a small shed-like shelter at the rear of the officer's building. Joel hollered for Captain Holmes, pointing to the shed.

"Check out the shed, Harvey," Joel cried, then turned to the woman before him. "We will prepare any food we find there. We have eliminated any possible Japanese threat to the compound. You do not have to be afraid anymore, lady. We will defend this installation until help comes to take you to a waiting hospital ship in Leyte Gulf. Just tell us what we can do to help you, and it will be done. How many Americans are in the compound?"

"Most of the inmates are American and British. I'm an Army Nurse... I was captured on Bataan. We've been without food for days, Major. Food and water are our most urgent needs. We are losing friends and companions every day who simply lie down and will themselves to die. Some have been driven to another world all their own, and they may be forever lost to us. The beasts mistreated us in every way possible. Hope for liberation died a long time ago. We've lived with disappointment and inhuman treatment for so long it became a way of life for all those years..."

"We came as quickly as we could, Ma'am. God knows it wasn't soon enough, but we have never forgotten you," Joel answered in a gentle voice.

86

"Major, Major Thorn," cried Captain Holmes. "We've found a supply of rice and tea in the enlisted men's mess. I've got men preparing it now. Give us an hour and we can feed these ladies," Holmes was excited. "Oh, also. We found a water supply and a place where the women can shower in private. I have men fixing the place for their use."

"Thanks, Harvey, I'll spread the word," Joel replied, thankful for the good news. He turned to the Army Nurse. "Would you come with me so that I can speak to the inmates? Is there anyone in the camp who might act as a spokesperson for the group?"

"My name is Nancy Field. I was a Lieutenant in the Army Nurse Corps. I've tried to maintain discipline and to cultivate hope over the years. I've failed more than I've succeeded, but the women have looked up to me for leadership. I'll help where I can... I'm weak from malaria, and the bastards have used all of us for their pleasure... This last encounter was brutal... I was tied to the bed..." she fainted and fell against Joel.

He called for help to make her comfortable. Several troopers came to his aid. "Thanks, men. Please look after her. I've got to speak to the others."

He quickly surveyed the open compound mentally noting the graves, open latrines, and the low-lying meadow where he had crawled through the grass. Outposts he could see were alert and well positioned. He would direct the air drop to take place over the portion of the meadow closest to the wire fence. He was proud of the detachment he had led into the camp. Now he could concentrate on caring for the inmates. He asked his first sergeant to try and locate shovels to close some of the open latrines and rushed to the shelters where he found a large stump to stand on.

"May I have your attention... Please, I want to speak to you inmates. Now that we have liberated the camp, you do not have to be afraid. No one can hurt you anymore. You are free. We are American soldiers, and I have a detachment cooking rice and tea for you. Please be patient a little while longer. I know that you desperately need that nourishment, and we will be honored to make it available to all of you. It's important that we know how many of you are able to walk on your own and how many need assistance. We are here to help you so if you are too weak to get in a serving line to feed yourself, we will be pleased to bring the food to each of you in your shelters.

"The whole world is proud of the courage and sacrifice you have displayed after suffering inhuman treatment at the hands of animals in the Japanese Army. Try to put it behind you if you can. You are now free. Would those individuals who have acted as camp leaders please come forward? You can help us treat those most in need of care. Soon all of you will be transported to the coast where a large hospital ship is waiting to care for your every need. Until that time comes, we will continue to use the thatched shelters. I've had a few words with a Lieutenant Nancy Fields. She's being cared for."

About a half dozen women clothed in tattered shirts, pants, and some dresses approached Joel's position at the stump. They had much in common — sunken eyes that stared off into space; parched looking skin stretched tight against protruding bones; bodies that had lost an average of eighty pounds; and most frightening of all, they were going blind more and more every day that passed. They looked like small children except for their robotic-like body movements. Every tough paratrooper in the detachment fought to hold back the tears. It was a sight they would never forget. No one can ever imagine the degree of terror these inmates had to witness!

Joel plucked a tear from his cheek as he leaped from the stump. "How can we help you ladies?"

One lady stepped close to Joel so that he could hear what she had to say in her soft voice: "The women inmates in this camp were all captured when the Japanese took over the island. They are American or British. Some are wives of American soldiers also captured, some are civilian servants and school teachers and nannies to large families. Lieutenant Nancy Fields has been a tower of strength and personal courage. She defied the Japanese every chance she could and fought for better treatment. She was singled out and abused more than any other woman in the camp. We would not have survived without her strong faith in all of us... She comforted those who were dying and held all of us at one time or another in her arms to soothe our weak bodies and to strengthen wavering hearts..."

"Major Thorn," a burly paratrooper interrupted him. "The lady you called Lieutenant Nancy Fields just died in my arms, Sir."

Chapter Ten

"No, not Nancy," several women cried aloud. The inmates were stung by her death.

"She was a courageous lady," Joel said. "Those of you who have been inspired by her selflessness have a chance to show that you are worthy of her efforts. People like her will always be enshrined in your thoughts and memories. I will never forget this mission of mercy that has brought us here. The food will be ready soon. One of my men informed me that you women will be able to use the showers the Japanese troops used. I suggest that you eat some food first, then form into groups for the showers. I am hoping that the first drop of supplies will have fresh clothing for you after you take a shower..."

Suddenly the silence of the compound was interrupted by a flyover of two Mustang fighter planes wagging their wings at treetop height to announce their arrival on the scene. The planes ripped past them at high speed, then turned one to the right and one to the left and climbed to a higher altitude.

"Mustang One to Rolling Thunder," a call came over the portable radio.

Joel took the receiver from the radio man, "Mustang One, this is Rolling Thunder One. We are encouraged by your presence. Could you reconnoiter our flanks for any signs of the enemy?"

"This is Mustang One. We have already scoured miles around you and found no visible sign of enemy activity. Your request for supplies will be delivered promptly. We are riding shotgun for the supply planes. Do you have a preference for the drop? Mustang One, out."

"This is Rolling Thunder One. Please inform the transports to make their drops between the fenced compound and the meadow to the south. We desperately need the supplies, out."

"This is Mustang One. Transports are in sight. Will give information for the drop. Incidentally, we are going to support the rescue column that is being formed as we speak. Estimated time of arrival will be midday tomorrow. If you have a need for air support, call anytime. We are minutes away from your location by air. Mustang One, out."

Joel turned to the women inmates, telling them what the airmen said. "For now, ladies, prepare yourself so that the men can distribute food and drink to you. When the transport planes drop our supplies, be on the alert for some chutes that may fall near the shelters. The planes overhead are a symbol of the power our country is using against the Japanese. We are here to protect you, and to help you any way we can. Soon you'll be on your way back home. Be patient with us a little longer."

The lady who had spoken to Joel pointed to the women in the shelters. "Those who can't feed themselves will be paired with a person to help," she said, turning to

Joel. "We are grateful for you and your brave men. Over the years, hope was a rare commodity. It will take time and much understanding for that to take place. Hope has been shattered by despair. It's ironic, my name is Hope Larsen. I was a missionary nurse in a hospital when the Japanese came. My father was a Protestant minister. The Japanese killed him when he protested their brutal tactics. Here in the camp, I'm called by my middle name, Joan."

Joel listened to the lady with an eye on the horizon. "Then I will call you Miss Joan. If my eyesight is correct, I see our supply planes coming from the south."

Joan turned to look. "My eyesight is failing like everyone else in the compound."

Two DC-3 transport planes were approaching the prison compound at full speed. One climbed to a higher altitude and began a circular movement around the camp. The lower plane lined up with the meadow, slowing to a speed just above a stall, and dropped to an altitude just above tree top level. Suddenly the sky was filled with parachutes from bundles pushed from both sides of the plane. The meadow area was white from collapsed chutes. The first plane wiggled its wings in salute and climbed higher as it headed south toward the coast. The second plane circled and lowered itself for the same approach, dropping red chutes of ammunition and machine guns for more effective defense of the compound.

Joel excused himself from Miss Joan and ran with several men to check the supplies. He ordered a detail of men to distribute the machine guns and ammo to the perimeter security posts and to set the machine guns at both ends of the fenced area. Then he called for his platoon leaders to assign men to distribute the clothing which included men's underwear with tan shirts, pants, and lightweight sneakers for the inmate's cut and bleeding feet. Very few of the inmates had shoes.

After the women had been fed the first full meal of their internment, they were told that the Japanese showers would be made available for their use. Blankets had been hung on rope lines to make the shower area private for the women. Chairs were provided for the use of those who were too weak to stand alone. The soldiers carried some of the women into the shower area leaving them to the care of their friends. The gentle way the inmates looked after each other was heartwarming to the combat hardened veterans. The items most appreciated by the ladies were combs and hair brushes.

By nightfall, Joel and Captain Harvey Holmes were pleased at their progress. An accurate inventory of the fifty female inmates showed that twenty percent of them were too weak to walk. The stronger members of the group were quick to care for those less fortunate. No one suffered alone. The brutal treatment by the Japanese had strengthened the bond that held them together. Their second meal of rice and vegetables had been distributed just before dusk. The men saw a noticeable improvement in awareness of the women after they had digested the first full meal. This time, a treat was kept a secret from the women.

Joel asked Miss Joan to announce the treat to the women. She finished the rice in her small bowl and stood up from her bamboo mat. "Ladies, I have an announcement to make. The soldiers have saved the best for last. They discovered a supply of ice cream wrapped in dry ice, compliments of the United States Navy. Tonight we celebrate our deliverance from hell with the unexpected luxury of vanilla ice cream!"

The paratroopers saw an energized group of women shout and clap their hands. Ice cream in the middle of the jungle would have been a treat at any time. The men eagerly distributed eight ounce cartons with small wooden spoons to each of the ladies in the shelters. Small fingers eagerly reached out for the gift. Moist eyes accompanied their warm "Thank You" with weak voices. It was an experience those present would always remember with a tug at their heart-strings.

Joel watched the miracle that was taking place before their eyes. The showers helped to clean their filthy bodies, raising their spirits. The clean clothes were loose and ill-fitting, but they felt good against their dried skin. The combs also contributed to a deep sense of self. They sat quietly and patiently combing and brushing the snarled tangles of hair, while at the same time, a transformation began to take place within the close knit band of sisters. Hope was rediscovered, and it was accompanied with a sense of empowerment that was slowly lifting their spirits. The ice cream was savored by all. They ate it in small portions so that it would last longer.

Joel kneeled to speak to Miss Joan who was sitting on her bamboo mat eating ice cream. "It's gratifying to see what ice cream can do for morale."

"You can tell the U.S. Navy thanks from us for such a rare gift to our tortured palates," she exclaimed. "We are truly grateful for all of the effort that has gone into our deliverance. You have restored hope where there was a strong wish to simply die and not have to endure the trauma of our every day existence. It will not be easy to forgive and forget. Now, we have an obligation to those beloved friends who died horrible deaths in this jungle wilderness to live our lives and remember. They would want us to live for them, too."

"You've made us all proud," Joel exclaimed. "This has been an experience our paratroopers will share with their children and grandchildren, but they could never describe the courage and valor that sustained the women in this camp. Their survival is a just tribute to the human spirit. Few individuals will ever be asked to overcome the evil that the Japanese soldiers perpetrated against their captive audience.

"Well, Miss Joan, I've got to check on our outposts before nightfall. This will be your last night in the compound. Tomorrow will be an important day for all of us. Rest well, Ma'am."

"Thank you, Major Thorn," she replied in a strained voice. "Tonight, for the first time since we were captured, we can dream about tomorrow and beyond. Thank God you came when you did."

All of the outposts were manned. Joel took his place in the perimeter with his radio man, Corporal Jameson. He had a few candy bars to munch on during the night. Lieutenant Smart had informed him that the Filipino detachment was continuing their surveillance a mile or

95

so out from the compound. Soon the level of noise increased from the nocturnal creatures within the dense jungle beyond the compound.

A new day was born when Jameson gently shook Joel from a light sleep. "Excuse me, Sir. The commander of the relief column is on the line. It's Captain Snow."

"Thanks, Corporal," Joel said, taking the receiver. "This is Rolling Thunder One."

"Major Thorn, This is Captain Snow. I've just been given the task of escorting the relief column. We have my company from the regiment with us. The column is composed of Coastguardsmen driving five LVT amphibious tractors. We are on our way now, Sir. Estimated time of arrival is noontime. Have your inmates and their luggage available for boarding as soon as we get there. There is a Navy medical team standing by to receive the ladies. They have priority on Naval resources. The Coast Guard told me that they could take the ladies directly to the hospital ship anchored in Leyte Gulf just off the shore."

"That sounds encouraging, Captain," Joel told him.

"Oh, yes, Major. Have the inmates eat prior to our arrival and have blankets with them for the ride back to the coast. Captain Snow, out."

Corporal Jameson took the receiver from Joel. "Today is the big day, Sir."

"It was nice to know that Captain Snow is accompanying the tractors. He'll crack the whip, I'm sure, but from what I've seen with the Coast Guard detachment, they won't need any prompting. Come,

Corporal. Let's get something to eat and pass this information on to our ladies."

The camp was alerted to be ready for transportation to the coast. The cooks prepared breakfast of oatmeal with reconstituted dry milk, honey, and peaches. It was a nourishing meal and was easy on the inmates' shrunken digestive systems. Joel told the cooks to prepare rice, canned vegetables, and tea for lunch so that the ladies could make the trip out of the jungle on full stomachs.

Joel spoke to Miss Joan. "You should prepare the ladies to load the tractors immediately as they arrive. Tell them to bring blankets and any personal belongings they may have. We'll assist them into the tractors."

"I'll see that your wishes are followed, Major," she replied, having trouble lifting herself off the bamboo mat. Joel offered her a helping hand. "Thank you. For your information, Major, we do not have anything that we could call our own. Over the years, our personal stuff like purses all became lost or confiscated. I had destroyed my driver's license and identification card when I was captured. It was never wise to let anyone know our true identity. We were the great unknown who formed a sisterhood here in the jungle that has defied every form of human degradation the enemy imposed on us. Singularly, they defeated us. Collectively, we persevered, and soon we'll be returned to society where we will be complete strangers. We are anxious to make that transition, but to be honest, most of us are frightened that we won't be able to assimilate. Oh, God, no one can ever know how difficult those years have been..."

Miss Joan wept, holding her head in her child-like hands. Joel embraced her, feeling helpless. He shared her cries of desperation. It was true, no one could ever know just how vicious the Japanese were unless they too shared the decadent behavior. He gently laid Miss Joan down on her bamboo mat. "Rest a while, Miss Joan. May God in his infinite mercy comfort you and your friends who have endured a hell on earth. Thank the same God we came when we did. Rest easy, dear lady. Your days in Purgatory are over…"

Later, Joel received word from supporting fighter planes that a relief column was on its way and should be at the prison compound within the hour. It was good news for the hardy paratroopers. They assembled the women inmates in files along the edge of the meadow clearing. That way they could be loaded onto the vehicles without delay. They were far enough from the shelters and remaining structures so that the soldiers could burn them. The inmates cried out and cheered when the flames belched into the sky. Joel said to himself, "No one will ever suffer again from this camp.

While the women's fixation was on the burning camp structures, a line of amphibious tractors came out of the jungle like a large snake weaving in and around obstacles. The hum of their engines was like music to the ears of the paratroopers and the inmates who were witnessing a manifestation of their country's concern for their welfare. Each LVT had a driver and a gunner in a turret with twin fifty caliber machine guns. They circled so as to come to a stop heading back into the jungle close to the lines of wide-eyed inmates. Some were frightened by the steel monsters until the rear ramp dropped to the ground. Two Coast Guardsmen rushed to help the women load. They were taking the first step in a long journey back to their home roots.

The paratroopers quickly formed a defensive perimeter around the scene. Captain Snow approached Joel. "You did a great job here, Major. The Coast Guard detachment operating these LVTs borrowed all the mattresses on a destroyer in the bay so that the inmates will have a smoother trip to the coast. It will be a rough ride, but the mattresses will help some. The Chief in charge of the tractors has informed me that each tractor has a limited supply of cold ginger ale and drinking water on board for the inmate's use. They have made arrangements for the LVTs to bring the women directly to the hospital ship. They are very seaworthy. They are the most 'can-do' outfit I've ever seen," Captain Snow explained with a grin.

"I've had similar thoughts, Captain," Joel replied, checking the floor of the tractor closest to him. He turned to see how the ladies were being led into the tractors. Miss Joan was also anxiously surveying the scene with some apprehension. "There's room for all of you, Miss Joan. It will be a tiring trip, but the Navy hospital ship is waiting to serve your needs. We will accompany your column providing security through the jungle. No one is ever going to harm you again. May God bless all of you. Your courage and heroism has been an inspiration to me and the men. Bon Voyage, Ladies!"

The fifteen mile trek to the coast went without a hitch. At one point they ran into a group of Japanese soldiers fleeing the coastal region. Captain Snow's troopers quickly dispatched the Japanese without slowing the momentum of the column. The inmates were tossed about within the steel walls of the tractors while the gunner and driver tried to comfort them. Not one inmate complained during the trip to the coast. For years they had learned to suffer in silence. The fact that they were free and would soon be on their way to full health cultivated a dormant feeling of hope and thanksgiving. It was an awakening that did more for their spirits and morale than anything.

The paratroop regiment was ordered to Command Center for new assignments as soon as the inmates were safely delivered to the Navy. They were in for a few days of rest and relaxation. Joel was informed that their mail had finally caught up with them.

Few ever forgot the time when the LVTs came to a halt at the edge of the water on the beach. The large white hospital ship was clearly visible in the distance. The Coast Guard crews took the responsibility of safely delivering the women to the ship. They were caring and compassionate in keeping with their life-saving tradition.

Joel went to each tractor, climbing up on the tracks to look inside and to say good-bye to the women. They were obviously tired and apprehensive, yet there was a brightness in their sad eyes that he had not seen before. The image of thin, skeleton-like arms reaching up to wave a last farewell touched him. The last tractor was filled with those women capable of standing and sitting during the ride out from the jungle. Miss Joan was with this group.

He slung the Thompson over his shoulder and reached for Miss Joan's hands, holding them in his own. "This is the end of the trail for us, Miss Joan. The Coast Guard crew will take good care of you while being transferred to the hospital ship. The tractors can ride in the water like a boat, so do not be afraid. We wish all of you the very best. Go home now and put this sordid ordeal behind you if you can. You've all made us proud, and we salute your unconquerable spirit. The ladies were lucky to have you and Army Nurse Nancy Fields. God Bless you."

"How does one say thank you for being lifted from slavery to freedom? We will never forget what your men did for us. We shall pray for you, Major." She pulled him closer to her and kissed him lightly on the cheek.

The Coast guard Chief ordered the tractors to be started and to follow him to the waiting ship. Joel watched with Captain Holmes, fighting the moisture in his dark eyes.

"I don't know about you, Major, but I'm going to miss those ladies. They've displayed more guts and basic courage than any group of human beings I've ever known," Captain Holmes said, watching the small line of tractors churn through the deep blue waters of Leyte Gulf.

"I agree, Harvey," Joel turned away from Captain Holmes. "Let's see what the Command Center has for us."

Chapter Eleven

General MacArthur's determination to eradicate the Japanese presence in the Philippine Islands was rapidly evolving. Amphibious assaults against enemy strongholds were being conducted on a daily basis. Some days he had several underway at the same time. His genius as a tactician and strategist is obvious for the whole world to see. His use of amphibious landings, with air and naval support, were often accompanied by numerous paratroop assaults from the air to secure major strategic locations behind enemy lines. It was a virtuoso performance that astonished the world. He made more amphibious landings against opposing forces than any other Allied officer in World War Two. The Marines claimed about twelve landings in the Pacific. MacArthur made seventy-seven in his drive from New Guinea to the Philippines!

Joel and his regiment were to play important roles in the future. The regiment went into a staging area near an airfield in southern Leyte Island where they spent a few days resting and reequipping for another air assault. Mail was the first thing they looked forward to. Precious messages from home and loved ones gave the soldiers a moment to escape from the battlefield to a happier time and place in their lives. Morale zoomed higher shortly after mail call.

There were five letters from Inger, two from his mother and father, and two from Maureen who was stationed at the training center at Fort Dix, New Jersey. He spent two hours reading the letters, leaving Inger's for last. One from his mother was interesting. She had written that the local deputy sheriff had obtained the name and address of the person who owned the 1941 Ford Joel had seen at the Durham railroad station. The owner's name was: Athena Bell, 27 Baker Street, Portsmouth, New Hampshire. The deputy had no authority to inquire any deeper, because no laws had been broken.

Joel sat on his field cot and pondered the situation. The sheriff was correct; no laws had been violated, and he had no logical reason to pursue it any further. So much had taken place since the incident at the lookout that Joel hadn't thought about it until he read his mother's letter. He intentionally saved Inger's letters for last and arranged them in chronological order. The first four were full of wonderful chatter and gossip of local events and people. They brought a smile to his lips. He missed the home town and the security he always felt just being there. It was literally another world.

Inger was content with her position as a teacher in the sixth grade. She wanted to start in the lower grades so that she could eventually teach English in high school. She declared her love for him in every letter. Knowing that she was a person who vigorously guarded her privacy and personal thoughts, Joel felt privileged to be the object of her affections. He had no reason to doubt the authenticity of her declaration. He had known her since they were in first grade together, yet he could never say with certainty what she thought about certain issues. She simply never committed herself when she thought her opinions or feelings were irrelevant to a subject. Consequently, many looked upon her as being "odd' or "distant". It was her way of being herself, and he liked that independent streak in her. Whenever she said she would do something, she always followed through on her commitment, and she did it regardless of how others thought about it.

Joel opened the fifth letter, taking a long swallow of cold coke and read:

October 11, 1944

Dear Joel,

A short note to share some time with you tonight. The newspapers are full of stories from the war effort in Europe and the Pacific. I'm frightened for you and pray often for your safety and well-being.

My experiences in the classroom continue to reinforce my decision to become a teacher. Most of the students have some family member in the military. A few have had loved ones wounded in action, but none, so far, have had to deal with a death – thank God for that!

I had an interesting conversation with Jake Higgins when I brought my father's Oldsmobile to him for a muffler. We had talked about your experience on the lookout. Your folks had told me what the deputy sheriff had passed on to them. Jake recalled seeing a regular annual visitor to Lake Holly in the car with Athena Bell. He did not know her, but he knew that she was at the Lake every summer.

Perhaps she's one of the cottage owners on one of the more private lots at the western end of the Lake.

So far no one has come up with information about Athena's friend. It does not really matter now; the incident is past history, but you know how these small towns perpetuate and circulate rumors. No one knows the identity of Athena except you, your family, me of course, and the deputy sheriff. I can assure you it will remain our secret.

I've got a stack of papers to correct, so I'll say goodnight, my dearest Joel.

All my love,

Inger

Joel placed the letter on a field desk he had beside his cot. He had been feeling weak and sluggish all day. All of a sudden he had cold chills, and he began to shiver. Even his teeth rattled. He shared the tent with several officers. Captain Holmes entered the tent and found him on the floor in a fetal position wrapped in a blanket.

"My God, Major," he exclaimed, picking him up like a baby, placing him on the cot. "It looks as if you've got the malaria shakes." He called for a stretcher and rushed Joel to the small medical field unit at the airfield.

The doctors and nurses checked his vitals and began a regimen of quinine to check the malaria, glucose to control dehydration, and cold water baths to bring his body temperature down. He was not going to jump with his regiment any time soon. He was transferred to a larger hospital that specialized in caring for those soldiers that would eventually be rerouted back to their units. That first week he grew very weak and lost fifteen pounds. The heavy doses of quinine eventually suppressed the effects of malaria. The first week was the worst.

The Army doctor told him he would sign his fitness papers when he had regained the few pounds he had lost and he was certified by their physical therapist to be capable of carrying out any mission assigned to him. He promised to take the quinine as long as he stayed in the tropics. Release from the facility was something he diligently worked to obtain.

One day, two weeks later, one of General MacArthur's intelligence officers, Colonel Prescott, came by the hospital to talk with Joel. "You've had us worried, Major Thorn. The doctor tells me you're doing fine."

"I'm working hard to get out of this place, Sir. I've regained my lost weight and feel fine. This hospital is driving me nuts," Joel forcefully explained.

Colonel Prescott smiled at him. "I came to ask a favor. I need an officer to lead a couple of platoons against an airfield on the island of Noemfoor, north of New Guinea. It has been bypassed, but it is still a functioning base that is worrying our rear and our left flank as we proceed into the Philippines. Our intelligence has helped us to understand the situation. The island does not have a very large number of Japanese troops, but the airfield has become more active than ever. We need a small unit to neutralize the Japanese on the airfield."

"Are you looking for a volunteer, Colonel?"

"Yes," the Colonel replied.

"If it will get me out of this place, then you've found your man. Are any of my old regiment around?"

"They're active on Leyte right now. I assigned a full colonel to your position. I was prepared to promote you when I heard of your malaria attack. If you want this mission, I will promote you to a lieutenant colonel. You've earned it, Joel. I've seen what the troops think of you. I brought along a set of my silver oak leaves. They brought me good luck. I hope they do the same for you, Joel."

"Thank you, Sir."

Twenty-fours later, Joel and his troopers in two DC-3 transports were loaded for a flight to the small island of Noemfoor. They were heavily armed with extra ammunition for the Thompsons and the new M-1 carbine that some troopers were carrying. If they encountered heavier opposition than anticipated, a pair of P-38 fighter planes were assigned to them for close-in support. The planes carried napalm bombs and rockets plus their normal four fifty-caliber machine guns and a 20mm cannon in the nose of the center fuselage. It was an awesome flying artillery platform.

Twenty minutes after takeoff, they were informed the target was in sight. The men stood up and hooked their lines into the overhead bar. Each man checked the man in front of him to be sure all of his equipment was properly secured. They were going to make a short jump at about six hundred feet so that they could land in a cleared area beside the runway. A paratrooper was the most vulnerable to enemy fire when he was hanging in mid-air floating to the ground. Joel accepted the consequences of a harder landing to minimize the target they presented to the enemy on the ground. Every jump produced a few sprained ankles, but when veteran paratroopers jumped, their casualties were not any greater than those who stormed the beaches from landing craft.

Green warning lights began to blink. Joel was the first to leap through the door, quickly followed by the stick behind him. That silent lull he normally experienced was interrupted by a withering fire from the enemy below. The field below was alive with Japanese soldiers taking aim at the paratroopers. Joel swallowed hard and released the safety bar on his faithful Thompson. He pulled the trigger sending a short burst of fire into a machine gun nest below him.

Their aim for the clearing to the left of the runway was accurate. Joel landed in the area where planes were being repaired. He quickly shed the harness for the chute and surveyed their drop zone. He dove into a depression made by friendly bombers and yelled for his radio man to join him. Their first priority target was to capture the control tower and radio communications shack. Joel ordered the radio man to call in for air support to make a strafing run on the opposite side of the runway from their drop zone.

Two P-38s that had been circling overhead waiting for calls zoomed down to pepper the designated target area with 20 mm cannon and machine gun fire. Two napalm bombs were also dropped. Soon the area was ablaze with fire and dark clouds of smoke from stored gasoline and the gelatin gasoline in the bombs. Joel did not have to worry about any attack from that flank.

Joel led an attack to capture the two structures in front of them while the planes were attacking. That helped to keep the enemy down. About twelve men in a line threw grenades in front of them to eliminate resistance. The two structures were well protected by several machine gun positions with sandbags piled about two feet high around them. The paratroopers had gained an element of surprise while the planes were overhead, but they had just a few seconds to kill the soldiers manning the machine gun nests before they began their staccato of death. If they were unable to silence the weapons, they were in danger of being wiped out while they were still in the open. Several paratroopers were hit. They were caught in 'no-man's land'!

"Take cover," Joel screamed, throwing a grenade as hard as he could to silence the one gun still shooting. He hugged the ground looking for a way to flank the defenses.

The sandbagged trenches ran almost to the jungle. Joel saw that as an entry point and motioned the men to follow him. Crawling and dragging himself on the ground, taking advantage of several piles of crushed rock and sand, Joel then leaped to his feet and ran directly into the trench with his Thompson on full automatic fire. The machine guns were normally mounted and situated to cover the strip parallel to the runway. It would take the enemy a few seconds to relocate their weapons to counter an attack from their flank. They also had the problem of hitting their own men in the trench as well as the American paratroopers running towards them with guns blazing and grenades clearing the way forward.

When the dust and debris from the grenades settled so that they could see clearly, it was evident that they had silenced the enemy elements in the sandbag outposts. When Joel and the few men who had followed him arrived at the radio shack, they pitched several grenades through the windows eliminating any threat from the building. The control tower was next. He had not experienced any resistance from the tower. Once the radio shack was declared cleared, Joel motioned for the men to surround the tower. The tower was essentially an elevated platform with an enclosed hut on top of the palm tree poles.

They had no idea how many enemy were in the tower. They had successfully placed a ring of paratroopers around it. There was an eerie silence as the men took their positions with weapons pointing at the tower. Joel chose five men to follow him up the stairway to the elevated platform. He reached the bottom of the steps without resistance. His instincts told him that it had to be empty, but experience cautioned him to be careful. The minute he and his five men began their descent, a grenade was dropped in their midst and exploded.

Joel was thrown against a wall down the stairs. The two men directly behind him were killed instantly. The remaining three rushed past Joel, raking the top of the platform with automatic fire. The three Japanese soldiers were killed. The paratroopers then called for assistance from their comrades. Joel was peppered with small pieces of steel shrapnel in his back and legs. For a short time he was able to stand and move about. He was lucky to have survived the explosion. What disturbed him the most was the ringing sounds in his ears.

They had secured the airfield. There had been approximately fifty enemy troops left at the facility. He had his radio man call Command Center to declare the field secure. Soon after, two DC-3 transports landed on the strip with a P-38 fighter plane coming in right behind them. The control tower shortly had new tenants in operation.

A doctor came in with the transports to check on the wounded men. Joel was weakened by his ordeal but felt better after eating a ham sandwich and a cup of coffee compliments of a field kitchen crew. The doctor told Joel that the ringing in his ear could be from the concussion of the grenade. Joel removed his shirt and pants for the doctor to treat the small open wounds the shrapnel made, suggesting that he lie down to rest, giving him a sedative. The medicine made him drowsy and he was helped to a tent behind the tower where he fell asleep.

All night long Joel was conscious of planes taking off and landing on the newly acquired field. He was still in a state of unconsciousness, yet he had the ability to know that his ear had improved. He could distinguish the fighters from the bombers and transports. The next morning the doctor told him his inner ear had returned to normal after he had cleaned the dust and debris from the exploding grenade.

Joel left the medical tent to check on his men and the defensive measures taken around the center of operations until they were relieved of the responsibility by fresh infantry troops on their way from Australia. They remained in that capacity for a period of two weeks. He was ordered to turn over command of the area to an Air Corps colonel and take the fastest route to Command Center. He hitched a ride in a Navy Grumman Avenger torpedo plane to a base in southern Leyte.

He was pleased to be met at the airport by Captain Harvey Holmes. "Welcome to Leyte, Colonel. Those silver oak leaves look good on you. They're well deserved. Our old regiment is based here at this field. Two battalions are landing on Luzon as we speak."

"Hi, Harvey. It's nice to be back. I understand that I'll be your battalion commander. A Colonel Gibson has taken over the regiment," he said as he shook Harvey's hand. "I've gone from a regimental commander to a battalion commander and been promoted in the process. Who would believe what the Army could do?" he laughed at his experience.

Orders for the up and coming assault of Luzon were rapidly being dispersed with vast amounts of supplies and men being stockpiled for the occasion. General MacArthur wanted to capture the Bataan Peninsula north of Manila Bay prior to the recovery of Corregidor Island. Both locations evoked a great deal of emotion at home and on the front lines. The American Army had fought to their last breath. They continued without food or medical supplies for weeks before surrendering to the Japanese army. Their capture and treatment were collectively demonstrated during the Bataan Death March. The inhuman treatment of Americans became a rallying cry for victory. Bataan and Corregidor were important symbols for the Japanese and the Americans.

Joel and Captain Holmes were ordered to a conference in a large tent where they learned that their regiment was going to be used again for an air assault on Corregidor Island. This was the big one! They were given the task of securing what was popularly known as Topside. This included the old Army barracks, the large parade field in front of them and the famous Malinta Tunnels where MacArthur had his Headquarters section before being secreted out of the Philippines on a fast PT Boat. MacArthur's promise to return was manifested in the assault on Corregidor. Joel's regiment was going to be the instrument of destruction. This would be one for the history books.

Chapter Twelve

Joel took control of his battalion with his usual attention to detail. He knew that this next fight would be against a stubborn and fanatical enemy. The Japanese were losing the war. The closer the Allies got to the home islands, the more stubborn and fanatical their tactics became. They had a short time before the jump on Corregidor, so he put the battalion through a series of training exercises emphasizing marksmanship, basic infantry tactics, and a thorough review of how to control their chutes during a short descent of five hundred feet. The winds on Topside were strong and persistent and were capable of pulling a trooper across the flat parade ground over the sheer cliffs on the eastern side of the island. The lower they jumped, the better chance they had of hitting the proper drop zone.

General Walter Krueger was commander of the Sixth Army with orders to capture Luzon. The paratroopers were to secure Topside, while the amphibious troops simultaneously would land on the coastal shelf five hundred feet below Topside known as Bottom-side. The Navy would bombard the island two days in advance of the assault from the air and from the sea.

Joel warned the men to release their chutes the moment of impact. Otherwise they were in danger of being swept over the cliffs to destruction. He also emphasized the technique of throwing themselves off balance to the ground so as to not injure their legs or ankles in a hard landing. Hugging the ground and releasing their chutes made them better prepared to defend themselves against the tenacious enemy they faced. He knew that Corregidor would be a hard nut to crack.

The Island of Corregidor was shaped like a pollywog with a long thin tail. Their drop zone was midway between the tail and the head of the island which was only one-and-a half miles wide at its widest point and three-and-a half miles long. Corregidor was in Manila Bay near the famous concrete battleship known as Fort Drum. It is a small rocky island turned into a permanent artillery battery, bristling with guns.

The intelligent estimates passed on to Joel indicated that approximately five hundred Japanese troops were on Corregidor. He silently read the estimate and immediately dismissed it as most likely not true. Almost every engagement he had with the Japanese involved erroneous estimates. He wondered why the high command persisted in making them an integral part of every plan of action.

February 16, 1945, was the target date of the attack on Luzon. By then the battalion had absorbed the basic infantry tactic of fire and movement. He had also insisted on having a Navy fire control team with him so that they could call in artillery support as needed from the multitude of warships anchored in Manila Bay. He made certain that the field radio team and the gunnery officers on board the ships all worked from the same map with the same coordinates. Support was often on the way within seconds of the request. Their accuracy gave the troopers a strong feeling of confidence and security in knowing the vast amount of firepower available at their beck and call. They much preferred the accuracy of the Navy than of their own field artillery batteries.

The paratroopers were ready for the jump and received word to board the planes. He was the last man to take his seat in the cavernous transports. There was a confident air within the plane, but Joel knew that each man, including himself, looked from side to side wondering which ones would be missing from their ranks after the object was secured. Twenty-four hours later, some of the men would be lost to the world forever. Those losses troubled Joel even before they had taken place. It was that human side of him that made him a beloved combat leader of men. He sincerely cared, and they knew it.

The stick of paratroopers in Joel's plane sat in silence as it slowly taxied for position to take off. There were no wisecracks or jokes the way it was on practice jumps. The ride from Leyte to Corregidor was less than an hour. The drop zone was so small the planes circled over the target area until it was their turn to come in low to deliver the troopers. Joel was the first to jump out the door, quickly followed by the rest of the men.

The second his chute opened, Joel surveyed the drop zone below with terror. The parade field was alive with

Japanese taking aimed shots at the floating paratroopers. Headquarters had told him it would be a hard fight to establish a hold on the island. He agreed now, it was going to be an expensive slugfest. As soon as he landed, he looked for a good location to establish a battalion command post and serve as a defensive position until all of the battalion had landed. White chutes began to dot the ground while the air was still filled with them.

Joel located the hills where the Malinta Tunnels were located and called for his Navy radio team. Between his position in a shell hole and the tunnels, Japanese troops were firing every kind of weapon at the Americans. He called for artillery giving the Navy men the correct coordinates. In less than a minute the first shell arrived and the Naval gunner asked for a correction if one was needed. Joel told the radio operator: "Have the ships lay down a base using the same coordinates and ask them to lift the barrage at one hundred foot intervals advancing up to and into the cave openings in the Malinta Tunnels, and then cease fire until requested."

"I've got it, Sir," the husky Navy chief replied, sending the message. Joel looked around and stood up to scream as loud as he could; "Heads up to those who can hear me. The second the naval barrage hits ground, I want you to drive as fast as you can towards the Malinta Tunnels, mopping up any survivors of the barrage. Search for a place to defend and hold until the situation stabilizes itself. Follow me!"

The huge caliber of the naval artillery tore up the ground creating a massive dust bowl right up to the tunnels when the firing stopped. It was a wonder that

117

any enemy could survive the onslaught, but those that did soon met the fury of the advancing paratroopers. Joel spotted an old abandoned coastal artillery battery near the tunnels and decided to use it as a command post. The advancing troops took advantage of the cover offered by the shell holes so that they could regroup and plan their next move.

Seconds after the barrage stopped, Joel looked with horror. The Japanese came out of the openings in the hills by what seemed to be hundreds of men shouting and running towards them with bayonets flashing in the sun. It was a wave of fanatical soldiers bent on killing or being killed.

"Pull back to places where we can defend ourselves. Don't waste ammo. Let them come to us," he desperately cried aloud. He jumped into a deep shell hole and placed a supply of grenades on the rim of the depression, encouraging the paratroopers that followed him into the hole to do the same, and to place fresh clips into their weapons. They were in real danger of being overrun. His contempt for faulty intelligence grew stronger!

The screaming line of fanatic Japanese soldiers came within range of the grenades, just a few feet of the paratrooper's hole when Joel screamed for the men to throw their grenades as rapidly as possible. The carnage was beyond description, but the Japanese continued to run into the dust-filled barrage of exploding grenades. The paratroopers held their ground under the cover of full automatic fire. Joel had never seen such slaughter. His experience with the Germans fighting in Europe was different. The Germans would never have wasted valuable manpower in such a crazed mass attack. He asked himself why would any officer order a suicidal attack?

He considered falling back, but he noted a shrinking of the Japanese force and shouted for the men to insert full magazines into their weapons and to counter-attack the disoriented Japanese force. He leaped to the top of the shell hole, spraying an arc in front of him with his faithful Thompson. This was his first experience with the famous Japanese Banzai attack. The paratroopers stood their ground. Joel set the example emptying a magazine and quickly replacing it with a fresh one. He was hoping the Thompson would not fail him when it suddenly stopped firing — it was overheated!

He drew his automatic Colt pistol and one by one emptied the clip into the few enemy still standing. The field had been cleared of Japanese. The ground was covered with dead bodies. Even while they were handling the banzai charge, fresh paratroopers continued to fall from the sky. Joel thought, "Maybe the high command realized they were wrong about the numbers of defenders on Corregidor!"

Several men from Joel's battalion were pulled by the winds over the cliffs they had been warned about. Those who had remained airborne were able to land at Bottom-side unscathed. The ones who had touched ground on Topside close to the cliffs were pulled by their open chutes over the edge. Joel watched several fall to their deaths. He had his Naval fire team call for the pilots to make any additional drops at the edge of the parade field opposite the cliffs.

This engagement was one of the fiercest Joel had ever experienced. They had landed only minutes ago, yet it seemed a lifetime. There was one supreme act of heroism that he witnessed. Two enlisted men from his battalion, one a private first class and the other a first sergeant, had climbed the battered old flagpole still standing on the parade field and ran up an American flag. The Japanese Banzai attack had been underway while they struggled to climb the flagpole. The two young paratroopers were protected by Divine Providence. Neither men were touched by the shots taken at them by the enemy. They tied off the flag and let it unfurl in the wind. The whole battlefield below erupted in whistles, shouts of joy and claps that lifted the hearts of those who experienced the heroic act.

The tense battle continued into the night with little gain for the paratroopers. Whenever they destroyed a stronghold, more Japanese troops replaced their fallen comrades. That first night, the tempo of combat subsided slightly. The men were exhausted and tried to rest during the lull. Some ate from their C-rations and some smoked a cigarette; most simply closed their eyes while comrades kept watch for any enemy activity.

Joel could not rest. He had lost a large number of men. They estimated that they had already killed over a thousand enemy soldiers, yet they were coming out of the tunnels in large numbers. He called in for more Naval artillery support. The Army had not established artillery close enough for support of the islands in Manila Bay. The Navy had one advantage over the Army, they could use heavier caliber guns capable of blasting the island to dust if necessary.

The fight for Corregidor took ten days to completely eradicate the enemy from the island. Towards the end, the Japanese retreated to the tunnels where paratroopers blasted them with satchel charges. At the beginning of the war, MacArthur had placed his Headquarters and Hospital deep inside the Malinta tunnels. A maze of tunnels had been built in the granite hill. In one instance, several hundred Japanese soldiers had taken refuge in a tunnel and blew it on themselves so as to not have to surrender. They accepted death instead. Finally, after ten grueling days of combat, the last remnants of resistance were sealed in one of the tunnels by a massive charge of dynamite at the entrance.

Fresh troops came in to prepare the field for the flag raising ceremony with General MacArthur. The Americans had truly returned. The Japanese no longer held the people of the Philippines in bondage.

Joel made sure that his men were fed and received hot coffee, the miracle brew that all soldiers treasured above any other drink except beer. Their minds and bodies were numbed from the intensity of the past ten days. He learned from intelligence that there were five thousand enemy troops on the island, not five hundred!! Joel was too tired to be angry anymore. He curled up in a fetal position and fell asleep on the ground near the old artillery battery he had used for ten days as a command post.

The next morning, he was woken up by Captain Holmes who had a cup of hot coffee and a warm cinnamon roll in his hand for Joel. "You slept pretty sound, Colonel," Captain Holmes grinned. "Here, have a cup of coffee and a cinnamon roll I stole from the mess kitchen. It was one hell of a fight, wasn't it? I'm damned proud of the men. The battalion made us proud, Colonel."

Joel took a sip of coffee from the canteen mug. Before he could answer, Japanese soldiers streamed out of the ammunition bunker beneath the battery, throwing grenades into the clump of soldiers around Joel. He was lifted into the air by the explosions and remembered being angry that he had spilled the coffee all over himself.

Chapter Thirteen

Two weeks later on a hospital ship enroute to Pearl Harbor.

Joel came out of his coma with bandages covering his eyes. He could not see or hear anything, and he began to panic. He thought he had died, but then he could feel the gentle rolling motion of the large ship as it plowed through the dark waters of the Pacific Ocean. Where was he and what had happened to him? He recalled looking down at Captain Holmes who was motionless with blood all over his body. Then, blackness had consumed him. He had momentarily regained enough consciousness to hear one of the Navy radio men screaming into a microphone: "Medic...Medic... The Colonel has been hit bad..."

His body felt as if a heavy weight was sitting on him. He opened his mouth to try to speak and his lips felt dry. "Where am I...?" he asked in a weak voice.

A Navy nurse was standing over him with a moist cloth wiping his forehead and moistening his lips. "You're on a hospital ship, Colonel Thorn. You've been wounded, and we are taking care of you. Would you like some cold ginger ale?"

"Oh, yes. My mouth feels like a dried-up prune," he replied with a thick tongue.

She held a straw to his mouth so that he could swallow the ginger ale.

"Thank you, nurse." He laid his head back down on the pillow. "How did I get here? What happened to my battalion and Captain Holmes? Was he hurt in the explosion?" There was a hint of panic in his voice.

"I can't answer any of those questions, Colonel." She was reluctant to be the one to tell him how seriously injured he really was.

"I can't move my body, and I don't feel anything," he exclaimed in a weak voice. "All I remember is the Japanese came out of nowhere..." Joel struggled to say more, but the heavy sedation he was given relaxed his body and brought his breathing back to normal.

He had no way of knowing, but several wounded men from his battalion were also on the hospital ship. Captain Fred Snow, the officer who had led the relief column for the women prisoners was in the same ward as Joel.

A Navy doctor entered the ward to check on Joel. His conversation with the nurse was encouraging. The doctor listened to Joel's heart and made a notation on the record sheet at the foot of Joel's bed. He then went to Captain Fred Snow's bed. "The Colonel is responding. His pulse is quite normal and his hearing seems to be doing well. How are you doing, Captain Snow?"

"I've already accepted the fact that my right foot is gone. I can live with that, Doctor," he replied with a sigh. "I guess the Colonel and I have a ticket to the states."

"That's one way of looking at it, Captain. Tell me how the Colonel was injured. An officer of his rank doesn't normally operate on the front lines."

Fred nodded his head. "You don't know Colonel Thorn. He leads from the front, and he leads from example. The men in his unit would follow him to the gates of hell if he asked them. The mop up was about over on Corregidor when about fifty Japanese soldiers, who had been hiding for days in an old ammo bunker at an artillery battery where Colonel Thorn had established his command post, came rushing out to everyone's surprise and began throwing grenades all over the place. It took a few minutes to dispatch the Japanese before they had killed eight or ten of our men. The Colonel survived even though he was dripping with blood the same as our buddies. He was carried to a field hospital established on the island. I was taken to the same facility."

"I remember when he came on board," the doctor recalled. "He was unconscious and remained so until today."

"Just how badly is he injured, Doctor?"

"We've amputated his right arm. It was a massive piece of bone and tissue that could never have been repaired. His hearing may be impaired some. I was impressed that he heard what the nurse said to him in a normal voice. That could be one miracle for him. His right leg will require extensive surgery and long hours of therapy afterwards."

"I feel lucky by comparison," Fred Snow added.

"The ship received word that the Colonel is to receive a second Silver Star and a Distinguished Service Cross as well as a Purple Heart," the Doctor told him.

"He's earned any citations the Army offers him. His calm demeanor under fire is a sight to behold. His courage was never questioned. The thing the men liked the most about Colonel Thorn was the affection and concern he always had for the men. Respect came from the top down in his outfit. He was a good soldier, and the men he led into combat were lucky to have him."

The hospital ship was loaded to capacity and charted a course across the Pacific to Pearl Harbor in the Hawaiian Islands. One day Captain Fred Snow was sitting in his wheel chair near Joel's bed. He had lost a foot in the same explosion that had wounded Joel and killed Captain Harvey Holmes, a fine officer with two small children. He was watching Joel's hard breathing and came closer to check on him. Joel was moving his head back and forth as if he was in pain. His arm was strapped to his body so that he could not move it. There was a tightness to his neck muscles and his mouth was compressed as if he wanted to speak. "Do you want the nurse, Joel?"

Joel did not respond to the question. Fred called for a nurse, the same one who normally covered the ward, and told her what he thought. "It looks to me as if he is in pain."

The nurse checked his heart, pulse, and temperature. "His heart is beating rapidly. Would you please wheel out to call a doctor for me?"

"Yes, Ma'am." Fred left the room looking for a doctor.

Two doctors answered her call for help. They studied Joel for several seconds. "I believe he's having another malaria attack," one of them said.

Joel was heavily wrapped in bandages over most of his body because he was covered with cuts and abrasions from the grenade blast. The bandages had a tendency to raise the temperature of the body. They removed most of the bandages. Now that they were convinced that he was having a malaria attack, it became imperative that his body temperature be monitored and lowered. They administered maximum amounts of quinine intravenously, and began to bathe his body with cool saline solutions. There wasn't much they could do for Joel except control his body heat and pray that the quinine would work. The disease had to run its course. Often it produced lethally high temperatures. He was in God's hands, and they gave him a fifty-fifty chance for survival. The staff on the hospital ship worked tirelessly over Joel. They were dedicated professionals.

Every few hours Fred Snow wheeled over to check on Joel. The staff was doing the best they could giving Joel frequent saline sponge baths. In his delirious state, Joel repeated the words: "Inger... I'm sorry, Inger..."

Fred did not know how to interpret the words. Did it mean that Joel already knew how badly he was injured and he was apologizing to Inger, or was it something more personal between the two of them?

The paratroopers had been on the move so much that mail had not caught up with them. Everyone griped.

Mail from home was eagerly looked forward to. Now that they were on their way to Pearl Harbor it might be a long period without mail. It was one of the cruel fingers of fate that those who were wounded had to suffer in silence. They desperately needed the morale boost which letters from home produced. Their worlds and their futures were frequently altered by the wounds they had received. In that brutal world of reality, comforting words from home became a priceless commodity.

There was one consolation within the wards of the large ship. As soon as the men were carried aboard and inserted into the wards, they became members of a very select brotherhood. The wounded men had a natural affinity for those who were the most seriously wounded. They refused to let another soldier suffer alone. It was a powerful display of the heights that human spirits can climb. The sum total of pain and loss was greater in the wards of wounded soldiers than any civilian ward could ever duplicate. However, instead of gloom and despair, there was a tangible air of confidence and hope for the future. More courage and personal heroism was on display in the military wards than was shown on the battlefield. Their ability to circle the wagons around the most grievously of the wounded was instinctive within the brotherhood of warriors. Few civilians could ever understand that select relationship.

After a week of high temperatures and lapses of consciousness, Joel survived the ordeal relatively unscathed. He had lost a few pounds, but the staff was determined to put that weight back on him. He blinked his eyes and opened them looking into the blue eyes of a Navy nurse. "May I have a cold drink?"

"I'll be glad to get one for you, Colonel Thorn," she turned to Fred Snow with a big grin on her face. "Your friend has licked the fever."

News of Joel's recovery soon spread through the ward on the top deck of the ship. At first he asked for a glass of water, then ginger ale. Fred was at his side when he asked if he could have a cup of coffee and a piece of toast. It was a request the staff was happy to provide. It was an indication that he was improving and was capable of handling the truth about his injuries. The quicker he confronted the reality of his condition, the sooner the healing could begin.

It all started one morning when two doctors and a nurse conducted their routine checks on the patients. The head doctor checked his pulse and temperature and cleared his throat to inform Joel of his condition. It was not an easy task. "Colonel Thorn, we've stopped by to discuss with you just how we should proceed with your care. Have you looked at the charts hanging on the clipboard at the end of your bed?"

"No, Doctor." He was more uncomfortable than usual. "My body aches all over, and I can't wave my arms or move my legs. I think it's time I learned about my condition."

"You've been given the best medical care known to man, and you have the potential of living a full and rewarding life. Having said that, Colonel, we had to remove your right arm slightly above the elbow..." The doctor waited for his reaction.

"Was it really necessary, Doctor?" Joel asked in a trembling voice. His eyes filled with tears. Terror consumed him, and he was afraid... he was not whole...

"It was necessary, Colonel. You should know that we're also concerned about your right leg. At this stage of your recovery, we are optimistically hopeful that it will heal without serious limitations. The right side of your body received massive trauma from the exploding grenades. Penicillin has been a miracle drug in fighting infection. You have been getting maximum dosages of it. You should also know that your left leg and arm are not injured. We have fastened them to your body wrap so that you would not thrash about and further injure yourself. We can free them now that you are improving."

The nurse wiped the tears from Joel's eyes. "I knew that I was injured in the blast. I also remember being angry spilling coffee on me. Will you be able to fit an artificial arm on me?"

"As soon as your stub heals, we'll begin therapy. The answer to your question is yes. You'll be getting the best in the world, trust me on that, Colonel. You'll be able to lead a much more normal life than most of the men in this ward," the doctor replied forcefully. "Do you have any more questions, Colonel?"

"I've seen a lot of combat since I joined the Army. I'm aware that every soldier has the prospect of being injured or killed in combat. I can handle that. I've seen men in my command who have been wounded more than me. My greatest concern is, how will my family and friends react to my return home less of a man than went off to war?"

The doctor bent over Joel and looked straight into his eyes. "Don't go down that road of self-pity, Colonel, and whatever you do, don't look upon yourself as a cripple. Every human being has some limitations. They may be psychological or emotional, but they're limitations nevertheless. Hold your head high, Colonel Thorn. You'll be able to take on the world on your own terms. Your proven combat record has demonstrated courage and heroism few people can match."

Joel had taken the first step of his journey back to a life as normal as his wounds permitted. Recognition of his physical limitation was the hardest step of all.

The slow speed of the lumbering hospital ship traveled about a hundred and fifty miles per day. The ship's itinerary included a stop at the port of Bikini in the Marshall Islands where they would drop off soldiers that had improved enough to be rotated back to their units. They were hoping that mail had been transferred by plane for the wounded men on board the ship. They had earned a special effort on the part of the supply systems that supported the fighting effort. The staff on the boat said nothing about mail in case none was available. Then there would be no disappointment or false hopes. The ship's crew was pleased to load several canvas bags of mail onto the ship! The Army recognized the value of mail, especially for the wounded.

Joel was allowed to sit up in bed and use a wheelchair once the cast had been taken off his leg. He was monitored closely for signs of gangrene. The injured leg was broken in two places, one above the knee and another just below the knee. The surgeons did not like

131

the idea of a full cast on the leg because of the numerous cuts and lesions on the rest of his leg, so they settled on two smaller casts to hold the broken bones in alignment.

Writing letters home was a chore for Joel who was right handed. He knew that in time he would be able to write with his good left hand, but in the meantime, he asked the nurse if he could borrow a portable typewriter. He could hunt and punch one letter at a time. It was a definite improvement over his normal penmanship which left much to be desired! He was able to joke about it with his best friend, Fred Snow.

They had known each other ever since Fort Benning Parachute School. Fred was a tall, well-built blond with Swedish ancestry. He was easy-going and had a lot of friends. He handled his company of paratroopers by the book and shared Joel's habit of leading from example instead of command. Fred confided in Joel that he hoped to marry a girl he went to high school with in Needham, Massachusetts. He had gone to college at Boston University with a degree in journalism and a minor in ROTC (Reserve Officer Training Corps) and into the regular Army in 1942 as a second lieutenant.

Fred and Joel were playing cribbage out on the deck of the first floor. The sun was warm, and the soft breeze of the tropics was like a tonic to their senses. The ship sliced its way through the blue waters toward the large Navy Base at Pearl Harbor in the Hawaiian Islands. Ensign Adams, their daytime ward nurse, approached them with a smile and a handful of letters.

"I have a pleasant surprise for both of you," she announced. "We picked up mail at Bikini. I left some at your bedsides, and I have a few for you to enjoy out here in the sunshine." She gave each of them two letters.

"That was thoughtful of the Army," Joel said, accepting the letters. "Thank you, Ensign."

"Thanks," Fred said. His eyes lit up when he saw the postmark from Needham, Mass.

"If you two need anything, just holler. I'll be in the ward."

Fred began to open his letters and stopped to look at Joel who was tearing the letter open with his teeth. "May I help you, Colonel? In time you'll find ways to handle things like this."

"I didn't want to rip the letter inside, Fred. I'd appreciate it if you could open them and take the letters out of the envelope."

"It would be my pleasure, Sir," Fred replied, wheeling closer to the railing so that both of them could have a little more privacy. Two letters were from his fiancée in Needham. He checked the dates and wondered why they were so far apart. He read the oldest one dated January 1, 1945. It contained news from home. Several classmates were away in the service and away from home. One classmate that was in the Marine Corps was home on leave. She spent a lot of time writing about a New Year's dance at the old school auditorium. She wrote that it was a lot of fun. Fred was not interested in knowing that his fiancée was enjoying the company of a classmate on furlough.

Fred finished the letter and checked the post date of the second one. It was posted three weeks later. The first paragraph was one of the quickest "brush-offs" he had ever heard of. He cried aloud cursing her insensitivity and poor timing. Fred hadn't had a chance to write about his injury. He tore the letter into shreds and flung it over the rail. At first he was angry, then he began to cry holding his head in both hands.

Joel was a witness to Fred's reaction to the news from home. He wheeled his chair close to his friend and placed a hand on Fred's shoulder. What does one say to a friend who has been so traumatized? His immediate thought was that Fred had just received what became known throughout the country as a "Dear John" letter. "I can never know the pain you're suffering, Fred. Your friends know that you deserve better. How cruel and selfish it is to send a letter to a soldier overseas that invites such grief. Anything I say would not erase the pain, but don't forget, you have a legion of friends who care and will help you carry the pain."

"God-damn it, Joel. It really hurts. It hits you in the guts and explodes. If I had her here and she told me those things, I'd probably nail her one... I read the bitch completely wrong. We use to walk to school together for years. I never dreamed she could be so cruel and selfish."

Joel listened in silence thinking how his soldier friend had faced death with complete indifference and had earned the respect and affection of his company by being his unselfish and caring self. The Japanese could never have brought him to the state of despair that a single letter from back home had accomplished with impunity. Joel hated the woman who could do that to such a good man.

Ensign Adams saw what was taking place on the deck. She knew and admired how the wounded soldiers supported each other. She correctly assumed it had been one of the letters from home. It was not the first time she had seen a tough veteran of hard campaigns brought to his knees by unfaithfulness at home.

She stepped out on the deck and offered Fred a handkerchief. "Here, Captain. Can I help with anything?"

Fred looked up at her with red eyes. "Thanks, Ensign. It's my problem to solve." He took the handkerchief and blew his nose. "You Navy people have been swell to us. Everyone in the ward is in love with you, Ensign," he told her with an impish smile.

"That's the risk we nurses take. It's a common phenomenon in the medical field. It's also a healthy sign of improvement. Few people know how much suffering this war has produced. The courage I've seen in this ward has inspired me and everyone who has experienced it firsthand. Your 'girl back home' will never know, and she is the poorer for her lack of insight and compassion. You deserved better, Captain Snow. If you need me, just call," she said and left.

Joel saw the moisture in her eyes. "There goes a remarkable young lady. How could a patient not love her?"

Chapter Fourteen

A few walking wounded came by and visited with Fred and Joel for a while. Joel was getting tired and called for Ensign Adams to wheel him back to his bed. Fred remained on deck. Ensign Adams helped him make the transfer from the wheelchair to his hospital bed.

"Thanks Ensign. I hate to be a bother, but could you get me a cup of coffee?" he smiled at the request. "The Navy makes better coffee than the Army, so I better take advantage of it while I can. I understand I'm going to Schofield Barracks at Pearl Harbor."

"Yes, you are, Colonel. It's a fine facility on a mountain top with a grand view of the harbor below. Their physical therapy program is the best in the Army. You'll be in good hands. I'll be glad to get you a fresh cup of coffee."

"Thanks, Ensign. I'm going to read my mail."

"I'll be back shortly." She always brought an air of competence and concern to the ward. She never put on airs or was anyone but her natural self. Ensign Adams was of medium height with dark hair pulled behind her ears. She smiled a lot and was comfortable with who she was. Her respect for the men in her care was sincere, and the men knew that.

Joel sorted through his letters from Inger and started with the oldest postmark date. In that letter Inger remarked about his father's death and did not elaborate on it, assuming he had been told by his mother. He nervously fingered through his letters and found the oldest from his mother. Holding the letter in his teeth he opened the envelope and started to read:

January 5, 1945
Lake Holly

Dear Son,

Tonight I'm filled with despair and heartache. I'm saddened to tell you that your father passed away this past week. He was working on a construction job for the new Maine Turnpike when a bridge girder was being lifted into place and the chain broke. The girder landed on your father's bulldozer killing him instantly. I've been crying so much there just aren't anymore tears to fall. Your father and I shared thirty-five wonderful years together. He was my soul-mate and my best friend. I pray for guidance to help me continue without him at my side. He was so proud of you and the way you were promoted without any formal education.

Do not worry about me, Son. Jane is a comfort to me. She sends her love and prayers to you. The war in the Pacific is frightening. I can't imagine what you are going through. Maureen is still at Fort Dix. She's terribly concerned for you too.

Forgive me for being the messenger of sad news. Always know that you are in our daily prayers and will forever be in our hearts.

All my love, Son
Mom

137

Ensign Adams saw the same look on Joel's face that Fred had worn. Bad news from home! She shook her head and placed a fresh cup of coffee and a warm blueberry muffin on Joel's table. He was finished with the letter and dropped it on the table.

"Do you want to talk, Colonel?" she asked in that same soft way she had with every patient.

Joel looked at her. "It's my father… he was killed at a construction site. He was a bulldozer operator… Over here with the war raging all around us, it's kill or be killed. It's what we do to protect those we love back home. When death takes place at home it seems more cruel and personal…"

Ensign Adams saw his trembling lips and reached out to hold him. He wept like a baby in her arms. "Let it all out, Colonel. It doesn't help to keep it inside."

Joel was comforted by the release. She gently placed his head on the pillow when she saw two wheelchairs being wheeled towards his bed. She was touched by that instinctive quality that the soldiers have to protect and comfort one of their own. "How nice it would be if all of mankind could be so caring and responsible!" she thought to herself.

"The good Colonel has had some bad news from home. His father was killed in an accident," Ensign Adams told them.

Fred Snow was the first to speak. "News from home is not always helpful. I'm sorry to hear about your dad, Colonel." He nodded his head with a knowing sigh.

"I appreciate your concern. Thanks for the support."

"If this is what we get at mail call, I'm not going to pick it up anymore," Fred said with a light touch. "The latest news on the radio is that U.S. troops have captured a bridge over the Rhine River. They called it Remagen Bridge. It won't be long before our guys will be rolling into Berlin."

The fact that victory was within sight in Europe meant that more men and material was available for the effort against Japan. Fred had started a conversation that drew in a number of patients in the ward. There was a part of Joel that would have preferred to be alone. He looked around at his buddies from the ward and smiled. He knew what they were doing. They talked a lot about the future. Each of them had a different plan or expectation that had sustained them during combat.

Joel shared with them his plans for after the war. "As for me, I never had any formal education except high school. Just like most of you, I've checked out what they call the GI Bill of Rights. The government will pay for a college education. I think I'm going to take advantage of it to study forestry. I grew up in central Maine which is eighty-five percent forested with a large forest products industry. I could never handle a desk job. I prefer being outdoors. I even had my girl, called Inger, check on a curriculum at the University of New Hampshire just over the line from Maine. I'm pretty excited about it." Joel's enthusiasm for an education made the men think about what they wanted to do with their lives after discharge from the Army.

"If you follow through on your forestry dreams keep me in mind when you come across some good hunting and fishing locations," Fred good-naturedly reminded him. "I remember going fishing with an old high school friend in Central Maine called Lake Hebron in a town called Monson. I hated to leave the serenity and tranquility I experienced in the Maine woods. I think you've chosen wisely, Joel."

The gang of wounded soldiers in Joel's ward had become a very close band of brothers, sharing their hopes and dreams with each other. It was an easy thing to do because they had all been through the crucible of combat. That made their experience unique and meaningful. The long days on the trip from the Philippine Islands to Pearl Harbor was filled with the important task of rebuilding their bodies so that the future they talked about would have more meaning.

Joel's wounds were healing well. The stub end on his right arm was scabbing over the surgery necessary to cut the arm. The doctors maintained a steady use of antibiotics to ward off infection in his leg and arm. The smaller flesh wounds had healed and were no longer an issue with the medical team on the ship.

His leg was another matter. The doctors had to remove the two small casts when both became infected. They increased the dosage of penicillin and for several days did not replace the casts. They did immerse him in a salt solution very similar to sea water to help lessen the threat of infections they would not be able to control. Both of the breaks had begun to set according to the doctors.

When the ship was two days out from Pearl Harbor, Joel had a relapse and had another malaria attack. His temperature rose quickly, and he was in the throes of extreme heat and extreme cold. His body shook uncontrollably, and his teeth chattered. He was a very sick man. When the ship arrived at Pearl Harbor, he was weak and confined to his bed. He was slightly delirious when Ensign Adams said good-bye and wished him well. Army medics then carried him from the ship to a waiting ambulance for the trip up the hillside to Schofield Barracks Hospital. Once there they took measures to lower his temperature and to treat his malaria with a new drug recently released. It proved to work better on Joel than the quinine.

Joel had been at the Army facility for several weeks. His malaria was under control and would not be a problem as long as he never went to the tropics again. His right arm stub had healed better than expected. The Army doctors believed he was ready for a temporary arm, but delayed its construction until his leg was healed and ready for therapy. That way both parts of his body could be addressed with a diligent physical therapy program. Once therapy was over, he could be transferred to the states for fitting and therapy with a new arm. Schofield was responsible for bringing his body to that level of perfection where he could enter the real world with as few limitations as possible. He was encouraged by the prospect.

One day in April, Joel and Fred were sitting in their wheelchairs on a large terrace that overlooked Pearl Harbor. They could still see blackened and rusted hulks in the water. The USS Arizona was visible in its shallow water grave with several hundred sailors still entombed in the black hull. It is a powerful reminder of why the nation went to war with Japan. Joel and Fred were talking about the solemnity of the scene when an Army medic approached them with a serious look on his face.

"Word just came over the radio that President Roosevelt has died. Vice President Harry S. Truman was now their Commander-in-Chief."

"My God," exclaimed Fred.

The news stunned them. President Roosevelt had been an inspiring leader during the war. "He looked terribly frail lately," Fred said. "I don't know much about Harry Truman."

"Neither do I," Joel replied. "He might not make any difference. The conduct of the war is pretty much in the hands of the military. Hopefully, it will be finished by the end of the year. I'm anxious to get back to the states."

Fred turned to confront Joel with a serious expression. "Joel, can I ask you something as a good friend?"

"Of course you can."

"Well, I've had a couple of dates now that I can move about with crutches or a cane with a temporary foot."

"That's great, Fred. If you're happy, I'm happy for you."

"Would you say that if I told you it was one of the physical therapy nurses?"

Joel was puzzled that Fred should ask such a question. "There is such a thing as transference that can be a problem if carried too far between a patient and a medical person. You're two mature persons, so I don't see how anyone could object."

"What if she's Japanese?" Fred asked defiantly.

The question caught Joel off guard, and he searched for the right answer.

"See, It's not an easy question to answer, is it?"

"Don't prejudge me, Fred. I was trying to think how I'd feel. Would this Japanese girl be the Navy nurse that runs the Physical Therapy Center? I've heard that she cracks the whip like a tough first sergeant."

"She's the one, Joel."

"Is this just a date to help you change your mind about the girl back home, or is this a serious relationship? Is it the same for her? Don't get me wrong, Fred. I'm the last person to want to hurt you, but isn't this kind of sudden?"

"I understand that, Joel. That's why I needed to share it with you. Yeah, it may look as if it's too soon to know for sure, but I've never met anyone like her. I think she feels the same. She did suggest that we go our separate ways for a while. I agreed and we've done that. I have a feeling it may strengthen our feelings for each other instead of cooling it. You're due for therapy soon. It'll give you a chance to evaluate her. When you've arrived at an honest opinion would you share it with me?"

"I promise to give you the truth."

"Thanks. I feel better already. I have to confess, I've fallen in love with her. It was easy to do."

Joel placed his arm around Fred's shoulder. "Now, my good friend, what if the two of you discover that it's the real thing? What would your folks think? It's a hurdle you'll have to jump, and it may be a high bar."

"Would you go with me when we get back to the states to reinforce me with my family in Needham?"

"I'd be glad to, Fred. First, I want to complete the physical therapy course so that I can be transferred to Boston," Joel told him. "You know, I thought you were a little more relaxed and at ease with yourself lately. Congratulations, whoever the lady is, she's a lucky gal."

The Physical Therapy Center was the final destination for wounded or sick men before being reassigned to units or on their way to civilian life. Joel enrolled at the center and was assigned a room at the barracks and to a class of twenty soldiers and sailors. The Center was jointly administered by the Army and Navy and had the reputation of being one of the best facilities to prepare wounded men for civilian life.

"Gentlemen," announced a well-built pharmacist chief with a large number of hash marks on his left sleeve, indicating years of service. "I'm Chief Conray. Welcome to our Physical Therapy Center. You'll be going through a demanding series of exercises that will make new people out of you. At times you'll hurt and be uncomfortable, but believe me, the end result will please you. You're going to work together as a class unit. That means we help each other. The therapist in charge is Lieutenant Patti Tenaki."

The name Tenaki hit most of the men where it hurt the most. Hatred of anything Japanese had been so deeply ingrained that it was a natural response. Chief Conray held his arms out to a short Hawaiian nurse with long black hair down to her shoulders. She wore lieutenant bars. The disbelief, outrage and dark disappointment for some of the men was so strong it could be felt throughout the room. An ominous silence settled over the group. Someone called her a god-damned-Jap loud enough that she heard the epitaph. She ignored the rejection and smiled at the audience.

"I'm Lieutenant Patti Tenaki. I'm a registered nurse and a certified physical therapist. I want to help you mend the scars left by the war." She paused for a long time and slowly scanned the room making eye contact with each person. She never blinked an eyelid. Her petite build was enhanced by the white Naval Nurse uniform she wore with pride. She moved about at the front of the room with grace and dignity in the face of almost unanimous rejection and much hatred on the part of her audience. Joel thought it was in bad taste.

"I'm not a Jap," she explained calmly. "I'm a native Hawaiian citizen with Japanese parents. I graduated from Honolulu High School and have a degree in nursing from Boston University. Those men who object to me as their therapist may leave the room now and join another class assembling two doors down the corridor on the left. You may join that group with no questions asked." She continued to scan the faces of the group. Three men left, raising their voices in crude language about her ancestry. She watched them leave with a proud tilt of her head.

"Those who left the room have my sympathy and my forgiveness. I understand your distrust, hatred, and anger. If I were in your shoes I would probably feel the same way. So maybe, with your group, we have a chance to rebuild your bodies and shape your anger so that you

145

can direct it towards those who deserve it. Sure, I look like a Japanese enemy because it is my ancestry, and I dearly love my parents. If you knew them, you would like them, too."

"I have two brothers who joined the U.S. Army. They fought in Sicily and Italy. One was killed in action at Anzio. The other is fighting somewhere in France as we speak. He has proven his devotion to this country we all serve with pride. He wears the Medal of Honor, this country's highest award for valor above and beyond. So it's all right if you hate those who've brutalized you and your buddies. Just don't let that blind hatred rule your thoughts for others that have not harmed you. It's all right for you to dislike me for the way I do things or if I make mistakes or unintentionally hurt you, but please, I beg you, don't dislike me for my ancestry. You men have my respect, my admiration, and my sympathy for the horrors you've had to endure. I hope that over the period of our course I can earn your respect. All I ask of you is the opportunity to serve you. When we've finished the course, I'm confident you'll thank me and feel better about yourself."

The room was silent. She looked apprehensively from one side of the room to the other hoping to see acceptance of her offer. Joel saw an intelligent and compassionate young lady with a lot of grit asking for permission to help them heal their bodies. He was thankful to be alive and was glad to applaud her for taking such a courageous stand. He raised his left arm above his head and stood. "I have witnessed the heroism displayed by Japanese-Americans in Sicily. They are the most decorated unit in the United States Army and have endured the most casualties. Lieutenant Tenaki, you have my support and my admiration for your desire to serve us. Thank you. As you can see, I cannot clap my hands. I would if I could."

One by one the other men in the group followed his example. Lieutenant Tenaki was afraid that she had drawn a negative response and was nervously fingering the file folders she held in her hands. Then she saw Joel stand. She smiled and held her hand across her mouth like a little girl. Her eyes watered. She wiped away the tears with a handkerchief as the hall erupted in unanimous applause.

"Thank you, thank you," she cried. "The routines we're going to follow will be demanding, but we'll do it as a team. We're going to take your bodies and mold them back to their original condition. Our aim is to fine tune them into the precision instruments they were intended to be. At the end you'll be able to go out there and take on the world on your terms. One more thing before we start. I'd like the privilege of calling each of you by your first names. This is no place for titles. I have the roster list here and will familiarize myself with your names as we go along. Most who know me call me Miss Patti. You can call me other things but not to my face," she laughed energetically.

Joel had a feeling that this was going to be a fun session. Miss Patti was going to keep their butts humping very much like a tough drill sergeant, and she was going to do it with a smile and a laugh as she pushed them to their limits. He was prepared to run the gauntlet with the lady. He had a feeling that his friend, Captain Fred Snow, was making a good choice. Few families have proved the extent of their patriotism as much as Miss Patti's family.

Chapter Fifteen

Joel progressed through various stages of physical conditioning. The first few days he retired to his bed aching and sore all over his body. Miss Patti had them jumping, stretching, and running until they were ready to quit. She followed them in every move and seemed tireless. Her good nature and impish playfulness soon won the affection of everyone in the class.

The therapy sessions had become less and less of a challenge to Joel as time passed. His body and the injured right leg responded better than expected to the rigid routines Miss Patti put them through. One day, the physical therapy class had just completed a five mile hike around portions of the vast Schofield Barracks military reservation, returning to the center sweating and exhausted from their trek with Miss Patti in the lead setting the pace. They were greeted at the door of the ward by a jubilant soldier who hollered to them that Germany had surrendered unconditionally to the Allies. The guns were silent all over Europe! May 7, 1945 was a day they would never forget.

Joel had experienced combat in both the Pacific and Europe theatres. His memories of Sicily and Africa were clouded with visions of heavy losses and small gains. He was thankful that it had all come to an end. The war against Japan was inching closer and closer to the heartland. The Philippine Campaign was still in progress with heavy losses. It was an ugly contest that General MacArthur was relentlessly pursuing. Joel imagined that if the United States had to invade the home islands of Japan, they would end up killing all of the able-bodied males in the population, plus a large number of women and children. Japan was by choice committing national suicide. The cost to the United States would be beyond compare.

News of Germany's capitulation was cause for a celebration. Joel had ordered a new set of custom made tan summer uniforms that he had not worn yet. This seemed to be a fitting reason to dress for the occasion and celebrate at the officer's Club on base. He was still self-conscious about being in public without his artificial arm, but he was determined to not let it hold him back.

He had just finished showering when Fred Snow appeared at his ward in a new tan uniform. The Navy had fitted him with a temporary artificial foot. This would be his first attempt to wear it in public. Few would have known that Fred had been seriously wounded and had lost his foot.

"Hi, Fred," Joel greeted him, sitting on his cot putting on a pair of socks.

"Joel, I've come to ask if you'd join me in honoring this special occasion at the Officers' Club. I know that you've got a new set of tans. Let's celebrate tonight."

Joel hesitantly replied, "I haven't fastened my Lieutenant Colonel leaves on my shirt or blouse yet. Your offer sounds inviting, Fred."

"Sir," Fred placed a comforting hand on Joel's shoulder. "I would consider it a privilege to do that for you. I understand how you feel. Please let an old friend help you with your necktie and with the ribbons you have earned with audacity and courage. Those who know what they represent will look upon you with pride and say there goes a brave soldier who has sacrificed much for our country. Your empty sleeve will only reinforce that sentiment. Those of us who served under your leadership were fortunate. I'm proud to call you my friend."

Joel knew that Fred's praise was sincere, and smiled. "With a buildup like that how can I refuse? It'll be fun to get out of the ward. I will ask you to help me get properly dressed."

The two friends entered the Officers' Club at Schofield Barracks. It was alive with energy. Everyone was celebrating V/E Day. They looked for an empty table and found they were all occupied. Fred noticed Miss Patti and one of her Navy nurse friends sitting at a table with two empty chairs.

"Do you mind if we sit with our Physical therapy boss?" Joel asked Fred.

Fred gave him a knowing smile. "I don't mind if they want to share their table. The nurse with her is Ensign Cohen. They're good friends."

They walked towards the table squeezing past the crowded dance floor. Miss Patti recognized them and graciously invited them to share their table. "What a nice surprise. Gentlemen, this is Ensign Claudia Cohen. Claudia, this is Captain Fred Snow and Lieutenant Colonel Joel Thorn. Please take a seat. This place is about to burst. How relieved we are that the war in Europe will not consume anymore American soldiers."

"The Colonel and I wanted to join the festivities tonight. Thanks for making room for us," Fred said, taking a seat next to Patti.

Joel acknowledged the two Navy nurses. "It's been a while since I was outside of a ward in the public's eye. It's nice to be here. Do you have any rules about fraternizing with patients?" he asked, slightly uncomfortable about his empty sleeve.

"Colonel Thorn, tonight we're celebrating a great victory. If there are any rules or customs being violated, so be it," Patti exclaimed. "It's nice to see you in uniform. Your ribbons indicate service in Africa and Sicily."

Joel suggested, "Why don't we forget rank and just be grateful survivors for tonight?"

Everyone around the table nodded in agreement. "We all have much to be thankful for," Claudia Cohen added.

Joel answered Patti's correct assessment of his ribbons. "When you first spoke to my group in physical therapy you mentioned two brothers who fought in Sicily and Italy with the 442nd Regimental Combat Team. I served in several campaigns with them and can tell you first hand that they are one of the best combat units in the United States Army. Their courage and tenacity were a sight to behold. I'm proud to have served beside them.

152

You have every right to hold your head high, Miss Patti. They are the most highly decorated regiment in the Army. That statement says it all."

"Well put, Colonel," Fred said, turning to Patti. "Do you think I could dance a slow waltz or a fox-trot with this new foot?"

She looked into his eyes and smiled, "If you're asking me for a dance, then I accept. You'll do just fine, Fred Snow."

They made their way onto the crowded dance floor where Patti came into his arms. It was obvious what they thought about each other. Claudia Cohen was the first to speak. "Those two have got something special going."

"I've known about it for a while," Joel replied. "I'd ask you to dance, Claudia, but I feel out of place for now."

"Please, do not apologize for your condition, Joel. You'll see, things will be better when you're fitted for an arm."

"Where are you from?" Joel asked, wondering about her slight accent.

"I was born in Prince Edward Island, Canada. My family moved to Mystic, Connecticut on the coast twenty years ago," Claudia told him. "They have a magnificent buffet in the next room. Would you like to accompany me to sample some of their varied menus? I'm starved."

"It would be my pleasure, Ma'am. I'm starved, too. I haven't eaten all day. Would you assist me? I can't hold the plate and serve myself at the same time." he asked, following her to the large serving table.

She placed a comforting hand on his good arm and said, "That will be my pleasure, Joel. Just tell me what looks good to you. I'm going to try some macaroni and cheese with a salad."

"One of my favorites. I'll have that, too. I don't like to eat meat that needs to be cut. I do like fish because it's easy to handle with a fork. I'll take a serving of filet of sole, too. I see that they have grape nut pudding with whipped cream. I'm going to leave room for a serving."

They returned to their table to enjoy their selections. Joel was not as efficient eating with his left hand so he ate with a spoon whenever he could. They watched Fred and Patti on the dance floor. They were oblivious to the crowds around them. Joel had never seen Fred so relaxed and content as he was holding Patti in his arms. She rested her head on his chest. He was glad to know that Fred had found happiness even if it was not shared by his family. Fred was anxious to cross that bridge with them just as soon as they were transferred to the states.

"How long do you think Fred and me will be held here in Hawaii, Claudia? The wards are being overcrowded with the advances being made in the Philippines. You and Patti have done a magnificent job rebuilding our bodies. I feel better than I did before I was wounded."

"You and Fred will most likely be discharged within a week to a facility near your hometowns in the states. Most likely it will be Boston Army Hospital. You should receive word shortly, Joel," Claudia said, picking at her salad.

154

"My letters from home have been sent all over the Pacific. I recently received some letters dated Christmas 1944," Joel grinned, nodding his head. "I'm anxious to be fitted with my new arm. You and Patti have succeeded in bringing me to that point where I'm ready for the new arm. My leg is as good as new. Your routines have been demanding. Several times I was ready to quit, but your example inspired me to continue. Where do you get all that energy?"

"I appreciate all that praise, Joel. You and your wounded buddies are the source of our inspiration. How fortunate our country is to be served by such patriotism. The way all of the wounded warriors interact and support each other. It's a privilege for Patti and me."

The four remained at the club for a few hours celebrating. Joel and Fred returned to their respective wards to find their new orders to be transferred to Boston Army Hospital. That night Joel called home to inform his mother that he would be in Boston shortly and to hold his mail. He promised to call as soon as he arrived in the states.

Joel reluctantly said good-bye to the wounded men in his ward. They had bonded into a strong fraternity of brothers. Addresses and phone numbers were exchanged so that they could keep in touch with each other. The next day Joel had packed his duffel bag and took his place behind Fred for the bus that took them to the airfield. They were going by Military Air Transport directly to Boston Logan Airport.

Prior to his departure, Joel had stopped by the Physical Therapy Center to say good-bye to Miss Patti. "I don't have much time, but I wanted to say thank you for helping me come to grips with my wounds. Thank you sounds inadequate, but I really mean it. My friend, Fred, has told me how close the two of you have become. I wish you the best of luck in every way. He's a very special soldier."

Lieutenant Patti Tenaki was pleased. "Colonel Thorn, you've been a wonderful member of our therapy classes. Your support on that first day touched me, and I'll always be grateful for your decency and sense of fair play. I thank you for that," she replied. "It's impossible to keep a relationship quiet on a military base. I think Fred and I have a chance. Of course my racial heritage will always be a factor. He's been great about that. Today marks the first day of your journey back to a normal life. Good luck, soldier." She embraced him and kissed him on the cheek.

"Good-bye, Miss Patti. I'll always remember you." Then he left to catch the bus.

Two days later, Joel and Fred were roommates in a semi-private room at the Boston Army Hospital near the waterfront district. They were given a thorough examination and detailed measurements were taken for them to be fitted to the artificial limbs they would soon be using. They were also issued new sets of uniforms to wear until they were discharged from the Army.

They were restricted to classes every morning so that they could be properly fitted. Once the fit was obtained, they began intensive therapy. Joel's arm therapy was much more detailed and longer than that for Fred's foot. Most of the afternoons they were free to do what they pleased. Joel was anxious to get home to Lake Holly to see his mother and Inger. The Army would supply them with an unlimited gasoline pass when they did have time to make the trip. Joel was anxious to bring his Studebaker to Boston when he could get home. Shifting it would be a problem but he was confident that he could figure out a way of doing so.

Their first weekend in Boston, Fred asked Joel to join him at his parent's home in Needham, just ten miles away from the hospital. Fred was most anxious to inform his parents about his engagement to Patti and their plans to get married after the war. He was nervous about the discussion and was glad to have Joel with him for support. His gut feeling was that he could convince his mother that it was right for him and Patti to be together. His father was another matter, and Fred was afraid that he would cause a big scene once he was informed of his son's decisions.

Now that the war with Germany was over the towns along the Atlantic coast could revert back to normal and show any kind of lights they wanted. The regulations regarding lights at night were lifted. Those automobiles with half of their lights blanked out by black tape could have the tape removed.

Fred and Joel rode through the streets of Boston across Route 128 to the town of Needham. Traffic was lighter than when the war first started because of gasoline rationing. Joel was a little uncomfortable because he did not know what to expect. He knew his friend Fred only as he performed as a soldier and knew almost nothing about his family life except that he was intimidated by his parent's potential displeasure with his engagement to Patti. Joel did know that Fred was a graduate of Boston University Reserve Officer Training Corps (ROTC).

The wide thoroughfare through the center of Needham was lined with large elm and maple trees. The homes were larger and more expensive than those in Lake Holly. Fine homes with well-manicured lawns and gardens were passed by as they entered the residential portion of town. The cab pulled into a u-shaped driveway with a large entrance portico attached to the house with several chimneys.

"Well, this is where we get off, Joel. Back home you would probably call this an estate. My father bought this house about ten years ago when I was away at school. I was born and grew up in a much more modest home in Chelmsford, Mass."

"It's a lovely home, Fred," Joel said, getting out of the Checker Cab.

"Mother will be expecting us. I called her just before we left the hospital. It's great to be back."

The front door was opened by a middle-aged lady with long blonde hair pulled back hanging about her shoulders. She ran down the walkway and fell into Fred's arms. "Thank God you're home, my son," she cried.

"Mother, I'd like for you to meet my best friend and commanding officer, Lieutenant Colonel Joel Thorn. He's staying at the hospital with me," Fred said, releasing his mother.

"Fred has written often about you, Colonel Thorn. We're so pleased to have both of you home." Mrs. Snow embraced him. "You and Fred have been terribly wounded."

"It's my pleasure to make your acquaintance, Mrs. Snow. Our wounds are minor compared to many who have suffered more grievously."

"Come, you two," said Mrs. Snow, motioning them into the house.

Joel picked up his light duffel bag and followed them into the large foyer. He left his duffel beside a beautiful set of stairs leading to the second floor. The interior was filled with large paintings hanging on the walls. They entered the large sitting room with a small fire in an ornate fireplace. Mrs. Snow told them the maid would take care of their luggage. It was lavishly furnished, but it still had a friendly and warm air that made Joel feel comfortable. Fred took a seat next to the fireplace.

"My, what a lovely room," said Joel, following Fred's example and sat on the couch.

"It's a little more formal than I like," replied Mrs. Snow. "It's so nice to have you home, son. You're a little thinner than when you went to Fort Devens."

Fred was uncomfortable. He was hoping to bring up Patti before his father came home. "Mother, I have something to tell you that I hope will make you happy for me. Joel here has known about it for some time now."

"Are you in any kind of trouble, Fred?"

"No, Mother. While we were in the Army Hospital at Schofield Barracks I met a nurse and fell in love for the first time in my life. We are engaged and plan to marry

159

as soon as the war is over. I'm hoping you'll share our happiness."

Mrs. Snow listened to every word from her son. She was an attractive lady with penetrating eyes that discouraged familiarity. Joel watched her closely for a reaction to the bomb Fred had just thrown at her. "Why haven't you written to us before this? It's kind of sudden isn't it? What's her name? You say she's a nurse?"

"She's a Lieutenant in the Navy Nurse Corps which is the same rank as a Captain in the Army. Her name is Patti Tenaki. She's a Hawaiian."

"Tenaki sounds like a Japanese name to me," Mrs. Snow remarked with some alarm and discomfort.

"Yes, Mother. She's a Japanese-American and is a fine lady."

"My son wants to marry a Japanese woman while we are at war with Japan," she cried in a loud voice. "You can't be serious, Fred. Think of what your friends would think and say."

"If you will permit me, Mrs. Snow, Lieutenant Patti Tenaki is a wonderful person with a charming and engaging personality. It should be stated clearly that she is probably a more patriotic American than your neighbors here in Needham. I admire her tremendously. Her family has suffered great losses in the war," Joel forcefully reinforced Fred's position.

"The Japanese are the ones who have tried to kill both of you," she replied spitefully.

"I was hoping you'd trust my instincts, Mother. Joel is correct. She's also very good for me. You ask what my friends would say – I'd like to believe they would agree with me and wish us good luck."

Mrs. Snow sat in her chair watching her only son defend his position. She felt guilty that she could not share his enthusiasm. "Fred, all I want is for you to be happy. If this girl, Patti, does that, then who am I to object? This has been a surprise, and I can't help wondering what your father's response will be."

"I think of little else, Mother," Joel cried and started to walk nervously about the room. "I knew I could count on you, Mother. I can tell you with conviction, that even if father disagrees, I still intend to marry Patti if she'll have me..."

"And I'll be your best man, Fred," Joel added quickly. The atmosphere was beginning to get heavy.

"Oh, my son. How callous my reaction has been. I will not prejudge Miss Patti again. Forgive me. You're not a little boy anymore. You've proven yourself on the battlefield, and we're so proud of you. If this girl has won your heart, then I will trust your instincts and rejoice that someone has brought happiness into your life." She left her chair and hugged her son, laying her head against his chest.

It was a poignant moment for all of them. Joel was proud of his friend. Standing firm against the wishes of his mother and potentially against his father, too, took as much courage as he displayed under enemy fire on the battlefield.

Suddenly, the doorbell rang, and a voice was heard from the foyer. "Is my cousin home?"

Fred released his mother and ran to the foyer. "Cousin Athena, how nice it is to see you."

Joel saw Fred warmly embrace a slender woman with black hair done up in a bun on the back of her head. She was dressed in a plaid skirt and a blue blazer. She was obviously glad to see Fred.

"Your mother told me you had been transferred to Boston. I went there to see you, and they told me you had gone home for a visit."

"Athena, I came home with my best friend and my commanding officer, Colonel Joel Thorn. Joel, meet my cousin, Athena Bell."

Athena Bell looked into Joel's eyes for a moment and fainted into Fred's arms!

Chapter Sixteen

Joel winced at the look of terror in the lady's eyes directed at him before she passed out. He helped Fred carry her to the couch by the fireplace. Mrs. Snow rushed to the bathroom to get a wet cloth and smelling salts.

"What in the world came over her?" Mrs. Snow exclaimed. She held the bottle of ammonium carbonate near Athena's nose until she moved away from it and opened her eyes. "What happened to you, Athena?"

Fred kneeled on the floor beside the couch and took her hands in his. "Are you all right, Athena? Do you want us to call a doctor? You're frightening us..."

Athena shook her head. "No, Fred. I'll be okay. I'm embarrassed. I mistook your friend for someone else. I'm sorry. It's been a bad year for me. Please, I want to sit up."

"Here, my dear, let me help you," said Mrs. Snow. "Are you sure you don't want a doctor? Your mother told me just yesterday that you had received word from the Red Cross about your fiancée's gravesite in Germany."

"Yes, now we know that Donald was given a military funeral by the German Luftwaffe, and his remains are at a cemetery in Germany. The American authorities were notified of his death and received Donald's dog tags. They passed them on to me."

"I'm glad to hear that, Athena," Fred tried to reassure her.

"I'm so sorry for causing this disturbance, especially in the presence of your friend. I should be on my way. I'll stop by later..."

Athena was interrupted by a booming voice from the foyer. "What's all the excitement?" It was Fred's father, James Snow.

"Jim, we're in the living room. Our son has returned home. Athena just stopped by for a visit," Mrs. Snow called to her husband.

"Ah, so many young faces," he exclaimed, reaching out for Fred. "It's nice to know that you won't have to face the guns again, son."

James Snow was introduced to Joel, and they graciously shook hands. Athena quietly excused herself to use the bathroom. While she was gone, Fred's mother told his father that their son had something important to share with him. The elder Snow had a pompous and a spontaneous attitude that Joel did not like. He lacked the warmth that came natural to Fred's mother.

James turned to his son and asked, "What have you got, Fred? You look remarkably well considering what you've been through."

Joel had the feeling that Fred was a little intimidated by his father's superior air of presence. "Well, Father, I owe my good health to a Navy nurse I met at Schofield Barracks. To make a long story short, we've become engaged with plans to marry after the war. I've already spoken to Mother about it. Her name is Patti Tenaki, and she's Hawaiian." Fred paused to let that fact be digested by his father.

Athena quietly entered the room, taking a seat near the foyer.

James Snow looked at his wife and then at Fred. His eyes were penetrating and dark. "I'm amazed! Have you lost your mind, young man? We're at war with Japan! This can't be real... Is it, Mother?" he glared at his wife as if to dare her to disagree with him.

She lifted her head and straightened her shoulders. "I've heard Fred's story, and Colonel Thorn agrees that she's a fine young lady. Jim, he's our son, and he has to make up his own mind about what he wants to do with his life."

"But she's a Jap..." James Snow cried.

"No, Father. She's a Japanese-American," Fred explained, his voice getting louder.

"Same difference... Has she got slant eyes?" Fred melted under his father's onslaught.

"Jim, settle down. You're being unreasonable," Mrs. Snow grasped her husband's arm to sit him down on the couch.

"I hesitate to enter into private discussions as I'm a stranger in your home, but I am compelled to say a few words in defense of your son who is a dear friend. First of all, I'd like to say that Fred's choice for a mate is a wonderful one. Lieutenant Patti Tenaki is an intelligent and caring human being. Every man in her care fell in love with her, including me. Your son is the lucky one to have won her heart. I think they make a lovely pair. She's

165

a strikingly attractive young lady with poise and warmth that endears her to the patients in her care. Do not judge her on the basis of her ancestry, but remember it is most likely that ancestry that has made her such a fine human being. It's not my place to pry or to get into the middle of family affairs, but you, Sir, are completely wrong in your portrayal of Miss Patti, your son's choice for a wife."

James Snow's eyes exploded with rage. No one had ever spoken to him like that. He was prepared to defend his position with enthusiasm. He looked at this Colonel Thorn and saw the ribbons on his chest and the empty sleeve and decided it was no time to make a scene.

Athena mentioned that she was leaving and would return at a better time. Joel took note of her decision and turned to Fred. "Old friend, I also think it's for the best if I return to the hospital tonight. You have things to settle here with your family. I don't want to be in the middle. I thank you and your family for the offer of hospitality. I'll be back at some later date. If I've spoken out of line, I apologize. I only wanted to tell the truth about my friend's choice. If your cousin could drop me off at the hospital I'd be grateful. If not, would you please call a cab for me?"

Athena replied in a low voice, "I can take you back, Colonel Thorn. My car is outside."

"Thanks for the support, Joel. Your suggestion is for the best. I'll see you Sunday night," Fred said, embarrassed for the turn of events, but not surprised. Joel said good-bye to his hosts and quietly left the room.

Athena was sitting in her 1941 Ford sedan waiting for Joel. He placed his duffel bag in the back seat and climbed into the passenger seat beside her. She started the Ford and stopped at the end of the driveway to wipe her eyes and blow her nose before continuing.

She broke the awkward silence. "You were wonderful in there. My Uncle James does not take criticism lightly. You handled him just right. He can be a hard man. Fred's in for a long night." Tears continued to roll out of her dark eyes. "I can't believe that we've met again, Colonel Thorn. I was completely unaware until Fred mentioned your name, then my world exploded. Dark and ugly images flooded my memory. I was afraid Fred and his family would learn of our introduction in Maine. I apologize for being so emotional."

"Your cousin, Fred, is one of the best soldiers in the Army. Don't sell him short. He has nerves of steel under fire. His men worship him."

"I think you've described the cousin I've grown up with and have always found kind and caring. My mother and his mother are sisters," she told him. She was a careful and alert driver as she entered heavier traffic beyond Route 128.

The atmosphere in the car was tense. He had a suggestion. "May I be bold enough to call you by your first name, Athena?"

"If I can call you Joel," she replied with a smile.

A smile, he thought! "I haven't eaten all day. Would it be inappropriate to ask you to join me at the Officers' Club for a meal? I have a gasoline card if you'd like to fill your tank. I understand that rationing does not allow much traveling."

167

"I'd appreciate that. The Officers' Club sounds fine to me. I'm hungry, too. I was planning to mooch a meal at Fred's. I'm having a hard time believing what has happened. Ever since I wrote that letter to you, I've done a lot of soul searching. I'd like to believe that I'm a better person than the one you met on that lookout ledge. Embarrassment and shame quickly come to mind. The only person to know about our incident is a friend who spends every summer at Lake Holly. How often I've wished that never took place. I'm ashamed and still feel guilty."

Joel listened to her describe the situation. How strange that a year later, they meet again. "I have a confession to make. After the incident, I was curious about you, and no one in town seemed to know. The garage owner who pulled your Ford out of the ditch told me he thought your vehicle had New Hampshire plates. I was on my way back to the hospital by train when I noticed a green 1941 Ford four-door parked at the railroad station in Durham, New Hampshire. I got out to get the plate number. It was a remarkable coincidence. I then had my father and mother ask the local sheriff to check on the number. After that, I knew your name and Portsmouth, New Hampshire address. I'm not sure what I would have done with that information if we had not met at Fred's place."

"You must hate me for putting you through that ordeal after having been wounded. I hate myself."

"No, I don't dislike you, Athena. My combat experience has left me wounded twice, yet both times I survived when others did not. I'm so thankful to be alive and to have the chance to live a normal life even with an artificial arm. Many good men died on the battlefield. To be honest, my feelings for you were mixed. I was angered that any person could have the desire to end life, and saddened that you had been so overwhelmed with pain and grief that it seemed to be the only way out for relief. You were responsible for some of the events, but I'm not in a position to judge you. Every person has their own private hell..."

"I always knew that, but I was too consumed with self-loathing," she confessed in a low voice. "I wonder if you have a private hell..."

He had never talked about his sleepless nights and ugly dreams to anyone. This conversation with Athena was getting intimate. "I've never expressed it to anyone. Any soldier that has led men in battle knows what I mean. My nightly terror is images of young brave men torn to pieces on the battlefield in the prime of their lives. Were their deaths a product of my incompetence? The question that continues to haunt me is how could I have handled the situation differently? Sure, we had a mission to carry out, but it was my responsibility to get it done. Would different tactics have resulted in fewer deaths? I've never resolved that question."

Athena had just turned north onto Route One. She regretted asking the question. Joel was not comfortable sharing it with her. "I apologize. I've been selfish. Our conversation has only been about me and my problems. I thought I was the only one to be tested by the war. My life has been touched the same as thousands of other families. Most have handled the trauma better than me. I betrayed a wonderful love with a cheap, sordid act that has defined me. I don't think much of myself anymore. That's the reason I'm so bitter and short-tempered."

"Why don't you pull up to a station and let me fill your car's gas tank? I insist on paying. Please, let me do this."

"I'm grateful for the offer. Thanks for your generosity. It's been a long time since the gas tank has been full. How do we get to the Officers' Club from here?" she asked, pulling into a Shell station.

"It's on the waterfront near the Army Base. I think it's off Atlantic Avenue."

Twenty minutes later, Athena pulled into the Officers' Club parking lot. "I've never been in an Officers' Club."

"Well, this is your chance to try one. Traditionally, they offer better food than most commercial restaurants. I'll leave my duffel in the car until we're finished here," Joel said.

He held the door open for her, and they entered the reception area where he showed his ID card. They were escorted to the dining room where soft music was playing over loudspeakers. They were served coffee and water by a mess steward in a spotless white jacket. Joel pointed to the large buffet table at the far end of the room. The foods available would appeal to most tastes. The Club was about half full with members from all of the services.

"I'm going to try the roast beef and a side dish of baked beans, my all-time favorite. I see they have custard pie. I'm going to take a piece before it's all gone. Could you help me? I cannot hold my plate and serve the food at the same time," he asked.

"I'll be glad to do that. You just tell me what you want and how much. The choices here are fantastic. I'm glad you suggested this. I'm going to have macaroni and cheese and a salad," she smiled at him, serving his plate as they went along the line.

They returned to their table with full trays of food. "My Lord, if I was to eat like this every day, I'd be fat," she said good-naturedly.

"Me, too, but this will be a lunch and a supper for me. I lost thirty pounds in the Philippines. I never want to see another stinking jungle in my lifetime." He took a few bites from his salad and looked at her with a strained look.

"What is it, Joel?"

"Could you please help me again?" he asked in a low voice. I can't cut my roast beef. Would you please do it for me? I think I'm going to be a pest until I get my new arm," he laughed at himself.

How nice that he can joke about his limitations, she thought to herself. "Cutting your roast beef will be a privilege. Being here like this has almost made me forget how we met. I'm glad you asked me to do this."

They talked a lot about the progress of the war as they ate their meals. He learned that Athena had a younger brother in the Coast Guard in the North Atlantic. Joel told her about his experience with them and how much he admired their dedication and professionalism.

"Do you hear often from your family in Maine?" Athena asked.

He told her about his father's death and how he was anxious to go home to bring his Studebaker to Boston while he's being fitted for an arm. "Mother has been great writing. Her letters have been all over the Pacific following my moves from island to island."

"What about that special girl back home?" she asked hesitantly. "If I'm out of line, I apologize. It's none of my business."

It was a reasonable question to ask a soldier who has recently been in combat for a long time. "A high school classmate of mine, Inger, has graduated from a normal school in Boston and is now teaching at Lake Holly. She's been writing on a daily basis for some time now. I moved about so much in the Pacific with our paratroop unit on special operations that her letters are a little slower in coming."

"I'm sorry I asked," she said, understanding his concern about interrupted mail from home. "It's strange, you and I are really strangers, yet, I feel as if I've known you for a long time. I was ruled by a very deep depression for a while. Today I've felt as if I was released from the bonds of guilt. I thank you for that gift. I also have a favor to ask of you. Would it be asking too much if I requested that you remain quiet about our meeting in Maine? I want to bury that part of my life."

"Your secret is safe with me. I won't divulge what we've talked about; however, I have discussed what happened at the lookout with my family and a few people about town. No one knows your name except my mother and the sheriff. I almost spoke to Fred about my contact with a mysterious lady. I'm glad I held my tongue."

"On a lighter note, now that we've put the past behind us, what do you want to do after the Army discharges you?" she asked, glad to change the subject.

"Before I answer that question, I have one for you. You wrote on your note that you're a teacher. Where do you teach?" he asked.

"I'm a chemistry professor at the University of New Hampshire."

"I thought that would be the case. That also explains your car at the UNH campus," he replied.

"Actually, it was by chance you saw my car at the station. I normally park it at the department parking area opposite the ROTC building. That day I had taken the train to Boston. Gas rationing makes it necessary to take mass transit whenever possible. The fact that you saw my Ford in full view of passengers on the train is a strange coincidence!"

They ate their meals talking a lot about the forestry degree the University offered and the recently passed national legislation that became known as the GI Bill of Rights. Veterans such as Joel had a chance to go to school and get a degree with financial assistance from the federal government.

"If I sign up for forestry, would I have to take chemistry?" he asked playfully.

"Yes, you'll start with inorganic chemistry, an introduction course, which I teach. Then you'll be required to take an organic chemistry course taught by our very able Professor Harris who happens to be a renowned nutritionist. I have several forestry students in my class now."

"That's interesting," Joel continued. "The University of Maine offers a forestry degree also. However, it's a lot more miles to Orono than Durham is from Lake Holly. I was lucky to be promoted from a private to a Lieutenant Colonel in the Army without formal education. I really admired the way the West Point officers handled their units."

"Your family must be very proud of you, Joel. The fact that your superiors recognized the leadership abilities in you speaks very highly of you," she said, finishing her cup of coffee.

"May I take the liberty of asking you how you handled the news of the death of your fiancée, Donald?" He knew it was an explosive question. "I'm not trying to pry into your personal life, but I'd be interested in knowing how one handles notification of death on the battlefield. I've had to write countless letters to families informing them of the death of a loved one. I always knew that my letters were responsible for tearing a family apart. It was my most difficult task as an officer. I can't imagine what it was like to be on the receiving end of such a letter."

"How does one describe the trauma of losing a part of their life? Of course, it was wartime, and death is an integral part of the clash of nations. Just like every family with a loved one in uniform overseas, every mail delivery was an exercise in terror. My reaction was complete withdrawal from the real world. It was also compounded by my act of unfaithfulness which poisoned the news. Only you and my friend with a camp on Lake Holly know what took place after that.

"The pain and remorse simply grew to unbearable proportions. My actions and thought process had progressed to the point where you confronted a human being ready to hurl herself into oblivion. You stopped my moment of insanity. It took a while, but I think I'm a stronger person now."

She was getting emotional, recalling the sequence of events. He reached across the table with his good hand and clasped hers. She looked at him through a veil of tears. "I did not mean to dredge up hurtful memories. Forgive me."

She turned away to wipe the tears. "You know, this is the first time I've ever verbalized my actions without breaking down into an emotional wreck..."

"Lady, I think you're too hard on yourself. Forgiveness is a virtue we should apply to ourselves. I'm sure that our good Lord has forgiven you, Athena."

"I'm so glad I decided to visit Fred today. Otherwise, I would not have met you. This has been a good day. Thanks for being such a good listener. You've made it easy for me. I thank you for a wonderful meal and for a tank full of gasoline, Colonel Thorn. I'll be glad to drop you off at the hospital. Afterwards, I'm going back to see my cousin Fred."

She drove the Ford into the portico of the hospital and turned off the ignition. She got out of the car to shut the door after Joel retrieved his duffel bag from the back seat.

"Thanks, Athena."

"Thanks for a swell day, Joel. I wish you well," she said, embracing him and kissing him on the cheek!"

Chapter Seventeen

Several days passed since Joel's chance meeting with Athena. He was enthused with his new artificial arm the Army had manufactured specifically for his body. It fully encased the upper portion of his right arm and was fastened with leather straps around his chest and shoulders. The first time the therapists strapped it on him he felt more complete. He could move the arm up, down and around with his stub. Activating the tongs was accomplished by sensors driven by body muscles which he had been developing since his first day at Boston.

His ability to duplicate natural motions like a normal arm and hand was going to take time and a lot of concentrated effort. He was determined to arrive at that point as soon as possible. For days on end he thought of nothing else, driving himself to levels of commitment that exhausted him. He insisted on leaving the arm strapped in place night and day. He wanted to sleep with it so that it would eventually become a part of his body, not just an add-on.

While this intense therapy was taking place, he did not write letters home or to Inger as often as usual; instead he used the telephone to keep in touch. The last time he spoke to his mother he asked her to have his

Studebaker serviced by Jake Higgins so that he could come home on the train and drive it to Boston.

One decision Joel made early in his therapy sessions was a firm rejection of a hook on the new arm to replace his hand. He was dead serious that it would make him look like Black Beard the pirate. He joked about it, but insisted that he only wanted a tong which he would learn to operate as a substitute to his hand. That commitment filled his days, and as soon as he was efficient enough with the new arm he asked for a weekend pass to get his coupe at Lake Holly.

He was met at the train station by Inger who had purchased a used 1941 Pontiac five-passenger coupe with low mileage. It was the first time she had seen him with his new arm. He was proud to show her how he could open the small stainless steel tongs to pick up small things like a toothpick. His crowning achievement was to pour himself a cup of coffee in a mug and then lift it to his mouth to drink.

She watched him with blurred eyes. When he had set the coffee mug down, she wrapped her arms around him. "I'm so proud of you, Joel. I know how hard you've worked to do this. Your acceptance of wounds you received in combat have not limited you. That courage, determination, and commitment have always been virtues I've seen in you since we were small children. I love you."

He knew that Inger was not one to speak impetuously or without meaning. At times he looked at her and asked himself what was she really thinking? She was not deceptive or misleading, and she was honest to a fault, but there was something illusive about her that made him, and everyone who knew her, wonder about the depths of her consciousness. He always knew that she was a very private person and a deep thinker. At times, he felt she could read his mind. His mother had told him that she was beloved by her sixth grade classes and by the parents. That did not surprise him. There was an endearing quality about her that was partially defined by the fact that she was a loveable eccentric who was comfortable with herself.

Joel's mother had obtained new registration papers for the coupe. He was anxious to have it available for his use in Boston. Sunday afternoon, he was ready to return to the hospital and was going to drop Inger off at her school in Portland on his way. They went to a restaurant on the shore of Casco Bay and enjoyed the afternoon together.

"When will your course at school end, Inger?" he asked over a cup of coffee.

"Within a couple of weeks. I just received an offer from the School Superintendent about a teaching position in high school teaching English. I've loved my place with the sixth grade students, but I think the high school position will be a little more of a challenge," she shared with him. "What do you think, Joel?"

He looked into her dark eyes and replied, "That's not a choice for me to make, Inger. Whatever you're the most comfortable with is for you to decide. We both remember our high school English teacher, Miss Freeman. She was a wonderful person who introduced me to poetry when we were freshmen. I don't know if I ever told you, but when we were close to graduating date, I asked her for advice. You remember, I did not have money for college and my parents could not afford tuition and room and board. She suggested that I prepare myself for manhood by joining the Army. She was correct in suggesting that the world was about to explode in violence, and the country was going to need every able-bodied man to defend our place in the world and to free those who have been enslaved."

"I don't remember that, Joel. Her suggestion was typical of her. I loved her for her pragmatism and insight. She was my favorite teacher in high school. She once told me that I should never be afraid to listen to or act on the little voice inside of me. I was not a popular student in school, as you must remember. Sure, I had close friends, but social events and dances often made me feel inadequate. I shared that feeling with Miss Freeman. She gave me a hug and told me that popularity is a very fickle thing. Integrity and compassion are virtues that are universally admired and respected. 'Never sell yourself short, Inger Williamson.' I never forgot those words."

"I think our Miss Freeman described you perfectly," he said, grasping her hands across the table.

They spent some time traveling around Casco Bay and at the Portland Lighthouse. Joel wanted to get back to Boston before darkness and left Inger at her dormitory. It had been a pleasant interlude for both of them.

"I'll see you sometime soon, Inger," he said, turning off the ignition of the Studebaker.

She leaned over and embraced him. "It has been a nice weekend with you, Joel. Your progress with your arm has made us all proud of you. I've been wondering where do we go from here? I know it's probably not the time or place to talk about it, but I think often of what's ahead for us. You are my future. I understand your situation, and my heart is always with you, Joel. Are you as certain about the future as you used to be?"

Joel's heart leaped at the question. Had she read his mind about meeting Athena Bell? "No, Inger. I've been thinking a lot about the future, too. I'm not completely equipped to enter the workforce yet. College looks like a possibility for me. If I sound selfish and uncaring, forgive me. I'm not the same person you said good-bye to a year ago, Inger."

She embraced him. "Of course I understand that, and I want to support your every decision for the future. I just thought I detected a more distant and uncertain attitude from you this time. Forgive me. I never want to be a nuisance, and sometimes my imagination can be a nuisance. Thanks for the ride to school. I've enjoyed the day. You take care, Colonel Thorn. I'm so proud of you..."

He opened the door for her and carried her suitcase to the dormitory entrance. "Thanks for everything, Inger, but most of all thanks for being you." He kissed her waiting lips, and she ran into the dormitory.

He was a little troubled by Inger's question. Had she detected the secret he was keeping about Athena Bell? He felt guilty about that. The fact that he knew more about Athena's inner thoughts than he did Inger's fueled that guilt even more. He had to admit that there was something about Athena that made her look vulnerable, and he had an unsettling desire to shield and to protect her from the world and herself. Inger must have sensed that concern and acted on her instincts.

That night Joel laid awake and thought about where he wanted to go and what he wanted to do once he was out of the Army. Inger had touched on a subject that was important to the two of them. His immediate concern was to have the Studebaker coupe gear shift lever modified so that it could be shifted to any desired gear by raising or lowering the lever. He had talked about it to the therapist who had told him that it was a simple design change for a good mechanic. He was determined to have that done. His experience over the weekend with the coupe reinforced his decision to have that modification done. The next day he had a Studebaker dealership handle the job.

One day in the first week in August, Joel was prepared to take Fred home again when the hospital erupted into wild and boisterous cheers. An announcement over the radio sent shock waves across the nation. The Japanese had surrendered to the allies! The war was over, and the guns were silent! Thank God! The two atomic bombs dropped first on Hiroshima, and then on Nagasaki three days later, had been responsible for the act of surrender.

If Japan had not surrendered, and fought to the end when the Allies occupied the homeland islands, the cost in dead men would have been beyond comprehension. It is likely that a whole generation of Japanese males would have been wiped out, and millions of American men would join them in death. As horrific as the two atomic bombs were, the prospect of continued fighting would have reaped a far greater toll of human tragedy. Every soldier who wore the uniform was fully aware of the brutal task ahead of them. Now it was settled, and the world paused to heal its wounds, and for the first time in years, plans for the future could be entertained with certainty.

Fred and Joel joined in the celebration at the hospital for a while and then left for Fred's house. The city was alive with joyous people. Sirens snarled, church bells rang, and every one was blowing their horns at passing motorists. It was a day the world would never forget. Fred's parents had begrudgingly conceded to their son's decision to marry Miss Patti Tenaki once the war was over and their lives could begin with certainty for the future. Fred had successfully assured them that they would love her once they knew her.

Those who fought in the war and were left with permanent reminders of its ferocity were as excited as everyone else. Their celebration was public, but there was also a private release of fear, anticipation, and uncertainty that had been a private part of their campaigns against the war. A collective sigh of relief from that bondage silently filled them with thanksgiving. Joel could not forget those who had given their all in the struggle for victory. Their silent cries in the night would soon be forgotten by the world. Fleeting memories and joy of brief reunions would fade away. Only those brothers who shared the trauma would mourn and remember just how it had been. The rest of the world would soon forget that a way of life had passed beyond recall. It was a time for reflection about the certainty and the potential of a future.

Joel accepted the invitation to stay for the night with Fred. He was pleased to see that Fred was at ease and comfortable with the family. They celebrated into the midnight hour before retiring. He slept well thinking about what the world would be like. Most of his young adult life had been spent preparing for combat, fighting in combat, and recuperating from combat. It was a new world he was entering, and he wondered what kind of a role he was destined to play.

The next morning, Joel and Fred were treated to a hearty breakfast of pancakes, bacon and all the coffee they could drink. Before they were finished, the doorbell rang, and Athena announced herself. "Hello, is anyone home?" she asked, walking into the kitchen.

"Hi, cousin," Fred greeted her. "Have a seat. Joel and I are stuffed."

"Take a seat at the table, Athena," Mrs. Snow pointed to the kitchen table beside the stove. "Are you ready for some blueberry pancakes?"

"That would taste good, Aunt Lorraine. It's nice to see you again, Colonel Thorn."

"Please call me Joel. My days in the Army are limited. We have much to be thankful for today," Joel said, sipping a cup of coffee. "The pancakes are delicious."

Shortly, Mrs. Snow joined them at the table. Athena told them she had taken the early train into Boston to pick up some books at a bookstore. She was anxious to share the good news about the war with the family. She had recently stopped to see her mother who was an invalid being cared for by her father. Her brother, Allen, had called home to tell them that his new duty station was on a Coast Guard cutter based in Portland, Maine. He may be able to get a pass for a few days before another patrol in the North Atlantic.

Fred's father, James, quietly took a seat at the table accepting a cup of steaming coffee from his wife. "How is your father doing, Athena?"

She looked at her uncle with a serious frown. "He was okay yesterday. I can imagine what took place last night. Any excuse to celebrate... well, you know what happens..."

Joel wondered about that statement and assumed that Athena's father was an alcoholic. She seemed down and was quieter than usual. He had just filled the gas tank in his Studebaker coupe and made a suggestion to Athena. "Say, I've been wanting to take a look at the University of New Hampshire campus in Durham. If you don't mind, I could drive you back to Durham and you could show me around. Tonight, I could stop to pick up Fred on my way back to the hospital. What do you think? The recent improvements to the shift lever on the coupe make it easier to drive."

Athena smiled at his proposal. "It's okay with me. I recently rented an apartment in Durham so that I could be closer to my work. Your pancakes are delicious, Aunt Lorraine. If I go with Joel, will you excuse me for eating and running?"

"Of course, my dear."

Jim Snow took Athena's hands in his. "You know, young lady, we've got to do something about your father. He's beginning to get out of control. I wish he had stayed with the AA program a little longer. He improves a little, and then he slides back to the bottle. I'll speak to him. He's a good man, but he's wasting himself away on alcohol."

Athena's sober demeanor told Joel a lot about her. Home life was not pleasant... "I appreciate the support, Uncle Jim. He's getting worse. Mother's in a constant state of apprehension. Brother Allen left for duty with the Coast Guard after words with father and threatened him if he ever laid a hand on mother. I know Allen meant what he said, too. We do need to do something..."

"My friend Joel's suggestion for a trip to the campus sounds like a good idea," Fred added. "You know the University better than anyone else. I'll be ready to return to the hospital when you get back, Joel."

"Then it's decided," Joel replied, finishing his coffee.

Athena completed her breakfast and joined her uncle, Fred and Joel who were checking the oil on his 1940 Nash Ambassador. She embraced Fred and her uncle. "Thanks for helping us, Uncle Jim. Dad doesn't listen to us, but he does to you. Well, I'll put on my tour guide hat for Joel. Good-bye, and thanks for everything."

"Good-bye, Athena," her uncle said, opening the door of the coupe for her.

They traveled north on Route One up to Portsmouth, N.H., where they turned left onto Route 16, the major route into the White Mountains. It took them about an hour and a half to get to the village of Durham. Athena pointed to a large house with a porch on the main street through the town. "I rent a small apartment in that house. It's owned by an elderly couple, and I'm the only tenant."

"Being close to the campus is important. I'm afraid this gas card will spoil me," he exclaimed, checking the town's center. "Now that the war is over, rationing will be relaxed for gasoline and foodstuff like sugar and meats."

She had him drive slowly through the main route pointing out the school's cafeteria and dormitories on the left. "Up the rise on the left is the student building called the Notch and then the library. Further from the road is Hood House, the school's dispensary. The large building with the tower is Thompson Hall, the main administrative center. It is referred to as T-Hall."

As they approached the railroad station, Athena directed him to turn left onto the street. She pointed to the Agricultural building on the right and to the creamery that processed the school's dairy products. She had him stop for an ice cream. They got out and had one of the tastiest ice cream cones he had ever eaten. "This is a delicious chocolate ice cream. They must make it out of pure cream."

She smiled and pointed across the street. "That is the building I work in. The ROTC headquarters is beside the creamery here."

Joel was surprised at the small number of students on campus. They finished their ice cream cones and continued down past the main heat source for all of the various buildings on campus. The industrial building had a large smoke stack that towered over all of the buildings. Directly across the street was the wooden forestry building. The University offered a Bachelor of Science degree in Forestry. It was a reflection of the importance of the forest resources in the state. Professor Clark Stevens was head of the department. He had a reputation of being an excellent teacher in the classroom.

"I like the man, but between you and me, he's a little bit of a flirt," Athena laughed. It was the first time he had heard her laugh.

"Somehow that doesn't seem to fit the image I have of how a forestry professor should conduct himself. I had two foresters in my regiment. Both were platoon leaders from ROTC. They were good men with both feet solidly on the ground. I relied on them a lot. They both struck me as being gentlemen from the old school."

She smiled at him. "Your notion of them is correct. As a group, they are some of the more serious and unpretentious students on campus. Now as we continue past the forestry building, the large new structure on the right is Kingsbury Hall, the engineering department. Beyond that is an area of new construction of small family quarters for the influx of new students, such as you, who will be taking advantage of the offer to educate themselves. The dormitories on the left are known as the Quadrangle. They were built during the First World War. That completes our tour. The school has a brisk athletic program and an extensive outreach program within the state."

"If I were to attend the university, living in a dormitory with a lot of teenagers does not appeal to me," he mentioned, thinking out loud.

"There are a number of private homes around the village who would like to take in a mature student like you. I could help you locate a suitable place."

"I'd appreciate that, Athena," he replied. "I'm not sure when the Army will discharge me, and I don't know what's involved in getting school grants. I doubt I could make it for the fall semester," Joel said, checking his watch. "It's noontime. Do you know of a spot to have lunch?"

She was pleased with the suggestion and had him drive back through the village of Durham towards Dover to an Italian restaurant. It was a favorite for faculty members, she told him. They shared a loaded pizza with cold pink lemonade for a drink. They talked a lot about study habits and routines that made a college experience more meaningful.

Joel was curious about her home life and asked if her father was an alcoholic.

She hesitated to speak about problems that close to her. "You heard Uncle Jim speak about my father. Yes, he has a drinking problem. My mother said he came out of the First World War with a taste for alcohol. Since then it has been a problem but not on a continuous basis. He was a historian and taught high school at Portsmouth. A few years ago, he was relieved of that position and has been bad ever since. He needs help, but it has to begin with him. No one can do it for him."

189

Joel apologized. "I'm sorry, Athena. I didn't mean to pry."

He drove from the restaurant and turned into the house where she rented an apartment. He turned off the ignition and went around the car to open her door. "It's been a swell day, Athena. Thanks for being so helpful."

She looked up into his eyes. "Thank you, Joel. I've enjoyed the day. Good luck in Boston." Joel embraced her and kissed the lips she raised to him. It was a moment of discovery for both of them.

He began to speak. She placed a soft finger to his lips and said, "Please, I want to remember this moment." She then rushed to the door and disappeared.

Chapter Eighteen

Eight Months Later – Spring 1946

Joel watched the restless sea attack the granite coast. In time the granite would be reduced to fine particles of sand, but it would take thousands of years. Sitting on the rocks at the Nubble Lighthouse in York, he was searching for some way of bringing order into his life. Now it was filled with turmoil and discontent. When he was discharged from the Army, he had great expectations for the future. He had mastered the intricacies of operating his new artificial arm and had learned to write with his left hand as legibly as he ever did with his former right hand. Much of his discontent was self-inflicted, and he did not know how to resolve the predicament he had created without causing even more hurt and pain.

He was registered in the forestry curriculum with boarding arrangements at a private home on Madbury Road near the campus. Athena had helped him locate the small apartment. The second semester at the University of New Hampshire started in February when he was discharged from the hospital and the Army. His disability payments were determined to be forty percent of his salary as a lieutenant colonel.

As he came to know Athena better, the greater the attraction for each other became. The speed and intensity of the infatuation caught both of them by surprise. In the meantime, he had sheltered Inger from the truth about what was taking place. It was horribly unfair to her. Inger had taken the train to Boston to visit with him several times that summer. Each visit became more and more uncomfortable for him. He was living a lie, and he hated it. His reluctance to inform Inger about his true feelings for Athena continued. He honestly believed that he loved two women at the same time!

The day he had confronted her with the truth, shamed him and hurt for a long, long time. How cowardly he had used someone who had always treated him with compassion and unqualified love and devotion. She deserved better. All he could do was tell the truth about him and Athena. He had harbored quilt for too long. He remembered that meeting with Inger with a clarity shared by few events in his life.

Joel had driven home to Lake Holly on Friday midday with the intention of meeting with Inger at the high school. He drove to his old home to drop off his duffel bag first, and waited until late in the afternoon when classes had been dismissed. Right now, Inger deserved the truth even though he knew it was going to ruin a lifetime relationship that he had cherished...

The high school parking lot was empty except for Inger's Pontiac coupe. He turned off the ignition key with his new arm and had difficulty because he was shaking all over. Confronting Inger with the truth was the most difficult task he had ever undertaken. He had spent four years at the Lake Holly High School and knew every room intimately. The view of Lake Holly was spectacular from the school. The sun was hanging over the White Mountains in the west, sending orange and red rays of light across the rippling water of the Lake.

He paused and prayed for guidance and asked himself if this was what he really wanted to do. Did Inger really come off as second best? How could he throw the relationship they had shared over the years into the ash heap of despair? Uncertainty overwhelmed him, along with a reluctance to inflict the hurt that would be the product of his visit. He slowly walked to the classroom that had traditionally been the homeroom of the senior class.

Inger was sitting at the desk in front of the room. She was correcting papers and was unaware of his presence. He swallowed hard and watched her for a few seconds. She was lovely. She had the habit of intensely concentrating on things. He had often seen that part of her over the years. How he wished for this mission to pass him by.

The first step he made into the classroom broke Inger's reverie. She looked up, saw him, and leaped from the desk running towards him with open arms. To hold her again was a cruel and bitter experience. At that moment, he detested himself for gross duplicity. She kissed him on the lips and looked into his eyes.

"Joel, what a nice surprise. I've been worried about you," she exclaimed. "The last time I saw you in Boston, I left with a heavy heart. All of a sudden, you've become distant and indifferent almost as if you did not care about anything. What's wrong, Joel?" She released him and had him take a seat at one of the desks.

He knew that she was intuitive enough to pick up on his moods and thoughts. Praying for the right words to say, he sat down. He was a little unsteady on his feet. "Inger, this is not the place to talk. Would you please take a ride with me?" His demeanor was stern and uncertain.

"If that's what you want. I'll lock up after us," she said calmly.

"This place brings back a lot of memories, doesn't it?" he asked.

"I was intimidated by those memories on my first few days of teaching here. I'm glad I made the change to high school. It's been right for me. You look as if you've lost some weight, Joel."

Joel cried to himself; "My God, am I insane to carry out such an act of cruelty to this wonderful lady who has done nothing but give of herself? I must be a monster..."

He avoided her perceptive glances as he held the coupe's door for her. They drove to a small private parking area beside the lake, and he turned off the ignition.

"Inger, there's something I have to confess to you that has been tearing me apart for several weeks."

"Are you..."

"Please. Inger, let me finish what I have to say, or else I'll never have the courage to say it again."

She folded her hands, resting them on her lap and said in a soft voice, "I'm listening, Joel."

"I know that you've seen a change in me. Well, something has happened that has turned my world upside down, and keeping it from you has been the hardest part... I've been seeing Athena Bell, you remember the one I met at the Lookout ledge. It was uncanny that our paths should cross after the incident. She's a cousin to Fred, my best friend. To make a long story short, I've fallen in love with her, and she's fallen in love with me." He turned to look at Inger.

She was silent for a long time as if she was distilling his words. "When did you stop loving me?" she cried through trembling lips.

"It's crazy, Inger. I've tried to figure out some way of telling you so that you wouldn't be hurt..."

"Good God, Joel, you're telling me that all of our plans for the future have gone up in smoke because you've fallen in love with a woman who is a virtual stranger to you? You're giving up what we had for that?"

"You make it sound cheap and wrong. I would never be telling you these things if I had a hint that it was not right. I can't love two people at the same time," he desperately tried to justify his position.

"I wish you and Athena the very best. I intentionally never pressured for your affection. I always thought it had to come from the heart, so I held back waiting for you to make that decision. Well, you've made it! For your information, I've had a feeling that we were finished. I never knew who, what, or why, but your whole persona had changed these past few weeks. Today's conversation is not as much of a surprise as you might think. I appreciate your honesty, Joel. What else is there to say? I

195

don't want to stand in your way for happiness." She opened the door and got out of the coupe.

"Good-bye, Joel. I know my way back to the school." She was crying and ran as fast as she could down a well-worn path through a wooded glen towards the center of town.

Joel felt a chill sitting on the rocky ledge at the Nubble Light, thinking about the last conversation he had with Inger. A Coastguardsman had already lit the light in the house. He had not seen or heard from Inger since that time several months ago. He kept his trips to Lake Holly to a minimum so as to avoid an embarrassing encounter. He could still remember every word spoken at their meeting. It left him empty and angry. Her words were not vindictive or hateful. She had taken all the pain and disappointment without a cross word and left the scene filled with anguish and a deep sense of loss. He never knew how severely he had wounded her. His mother told him that Inger was quieter and more of a loner than ever after the incident. She was always courteous and friendly to her and to his two sisters.

Athena was going to meet him at the Warren's Restaurant in Kittery for supper. They had both agreed to keep their relationship quiet. Relationships between professors and students were frowned upon, and she was in danger of losing her job. Therefore they were discreet and met only off campus. It had worked fine. Their love for each other seemed to grow, and both of them were happy when they were together.

It was dark by the time Joel turned his coupe into the parking lot several slots away from Athena's Ford. He entered the restaurant and saw her in a booth at the rear of the dining room. He casually sat down and was concerned for her. She was a nervous wreck with red eyes, and her face was as white as a sheet.

"My lord, what's wrong, Athena?" he demanded.

She looked up at him and began to weep into her two hands.

"Please, tell me... Maybe we should get out of here. People are beginning to stare at us!"

"I agree, Joel. Lead the way out to my car, and I'll follow."

He left a tip on the table and left the dining room as naturally as possible. Athena unlocked her Ford and climbed in behind the wheel. Joel rushed to take the seat beside her. "Can you now tell me why you're carrying on this way, Athena? Is it something I've done or not done?"

"No, no... it's not you, Joel. How does one explain the unexplainable? Just when you and I were settling into a wonderful relationship, something so unpredictable has come along and made it complicated."

"What are you saying, Athena?"

She cried into her arms on the steering wheel. It was a release she needed, and Joel waited patiently and apprehensively for her to find her voice. All kinds of ugly images ran through his head. He was concerned that he may have to take her home and was reluctant to do that in her hysterical state of mind. So he waited, placing an arm around her shoulders. "I'm here, Athena. You've got me worried, and I don't know what to say or do. Please try to control yourself."

She stopped crying suddenly and reached into her blazer pocket for a handkerchief to wipe her eyes. "My poor Joel must be concerned. Let me begin by simply stating that my fiancée, Lieutenant Donald Breck, is now in the Walter Reed Army Hospital in Washington, D.C."

"I thought you told me he was killed in action over Germany when his B-17 Flying Fortress was shot down," he was quick to state.

"I did, Joel, and I have the communications to prove it. I also have his dog tags the German Luftwaffe sent to the Army authorities along with their description of his military funeral and burial in Germany. Yesterday, I received official notification from the Army that he had been transported from a German POW camp to Walter Reed. The Army surgeons said that he needed additional surgery on his leg and arm before he could be discharged. Evidently he was wounded or injured when he had to bail out of his aircraft. The Army assured us that he's in fairly good physical health," she told him with a sigh of relief that now he knows.

"How do you explain that you have his dog tags and he's still alive?"

"I spoke to Donald about that. He said that he and the tail gunner of the plane landed close together on the ground and were taken prisoner by German SS troops. They were taken to a prison camp where they stayed for the duration of the war. Their dog tags were taken from them by the SS troops who must have sent them to the Luftwaffe who usually was in charge of airmen prisoners. The Luftwaffe generally abided by the Geneva Conventions and was strict in seeing that prisoners were given humane treatment. They gave notices to the Allies of the status of American and British airmen. Donald told me that the Luftwaffe must have made a mistake when the SS sent them his dog tags."

Joel was quick to realize that Donald and his family were the victims of administrative bungling on the part of the German officials. Someone had failed to "get the word." Snafus of similar nature troubled every army on earth. This new revelation was a frightening bit of information. He reached in the dark for her hand. "What are you going to do about this?"

"I'm taking a train tomorrow morning to see Donald. We were engaged to be married," she explained. "I never kept that from you."

"No, you were very up front about your life in that first letter you sent to me. That still does not tell me anything about us, Athena. Where do we go from here?"

It was a question she knew he would ask, and she could not answer. "You ask what I can't tell you, Joel."

"What do you mean you can't tell me? Do you still have feelings for Donald that overshadow feelings for me? You owe me an answer to that question, Athena."

"You're right," she answered in a wavering voice. "Let me begin by saying that I love you very much, Joel. My love for Donald was sincere, and we had made important plans to marry after the war ended. Maybe I love you and him, too. Didn't you tell me that you loved Inger and me both at the same time?"

199

The statement cut Joel to the quick. There was an element of truth to her statement. What could he say? The day Inger ran away from him had left an emptiness he was never able to overcome. For the first time since their parting, he knew how she felt. His world was turning upside down. Events were taking place that he was powerless to influence.

"I'll just have to let you make that decision. All I can say is that I'll be here when you return from Washington..."

She embraced him. "Thank you for being so understanding. I don't know if I should cry or sing for joy. May God help us. Regardless of the decision I may make, someone I care deeply for is going to be hurt. I feel sorry for that. Don't hate me for doing this to you, Joel. If you were me, what would you do?"

There was no evading the logic of her decision. "I'd do the same thing, Athena. It's strange how things worked out. I understand the gravity of the situation. It's wrong to wish that Donald had not survived the war. I truly admired those men who flew daily raids into enemy territory. I could never deny them the right of survival. Now, go, dear Athena. Do what you must do. Just promise to tell me the instant you make your decision. Will you do that for me?"

"Yes, yes, thank you. How easy it was to fall in love with you..."

He kissed her briefly and got out of the Ford. She started the engine and pulled out of the parking lot. He had a premonition that he would never see her again...

Chapter Nineteen

Three Years Later, Spring 1949

The graduating class of 1949 was sitting in chairs lined up on the athletic field of the University of Maine in Orono. It was a clear sunny day with a soft breeze sweeping the campus. Joel sat in the front row, pleased that the academic requirements for the Bachelor of Arts degree in Forestry had been met. It was the culmination of hopes and dreams he had entertained for several years. He found himself reviewing events in his life that had brought him to this time and place.

He was still stung by the rapid rejection of Athena. The day she left to see Donald at the Walter Reed Hospital he knew that the love they had shared was over. Yet, he continued to hold out for a positive resolution for he believed their love for each other was really meant to be. His first word from her was a letter dated June 6, 1946:

Dear Joel,

I had promised to let you know my decision when I had confirmed it to myself. This first visit to Donald made my heart sing. We had planned so

201

much and now it can be a reality. He was my first love and I cannot deny that it is still viable and real.

I'm sorry, Joel. Someday you'll find the one that's right for you. Donald has graciously forgiven my transgressions. I told him everything and the fact they did not destroy the love we shared was instrumental in my decision.

Forgive me, Joel. I know that I've hurt you and pray for forgiveness.

All my best,
Athena

He had prepared himself for a negative answer, but when it came he was overwhelmed with grief and anger. The outright rejection as if he had never existed was harder to accept than the loss of a friend, a companion, a confidant. A few days after receiving the letter, she telephoned him at his apartment. He answered the phone, "Hello."

"Joel, this is Athena. I'm calling to tell you that Donald and I are to be married in a few days. I was hoping you'd wish us happiness."

He got the message and replied, "Well, I care enough for you to wish you happiness. The fact that you'll find it with another man is hard to accept. I am transferring to the University of Maine to complete my forestry studies. It will be closer to my mother in Lake Holly, and I won't be an embarrassment to you or your husband. Good-bye, Athena."

He hung up quickly before she could respond. That day he left Durham, packing all of his belongings. There were no regrets in leaving Durham. A new life in a new environment would ease the pain he now felt.

Once he made the transfer to Orono, he took summer classes so that he could graduate in three years instead of four. The second summer at Orono he attended forestry summer camp training sessions. It was a change from the classroom schedules to practical applications of the tools of forestry. They were given a three hundred acre tract of forestland donated to the University as a gift. They did a perimeter survey of the tract and inventoried the woodland and drew up a ten year forest management plan for the tract. The concept of multiple use was at the heart of the plan.

Joel's sisters, Maureen and Jane, were sitting with their mother on the bleachers, proud of his accomplishments. He had gone home every weekend he was free and became closer to his family. Their support helped him forget Athena. The ceremony started on time with the main address given by the State of Maine National Guard Commanding General. Forty percent of the graduates were veterans. The roll call of graduates was called by the President of the University and the exercises brought to a close. Diplomas were handed out at the athletic field house where the graduates had to turn in their gowns.

A reception was provided with snacks and drinks at the field house. Joel had picked up his diploma and met his mother and sisters at the refreshment concession. He helped himself to a ham sandwich and a bottle of coke.

One of the first students to offer congratulations was a fellow forestry graduate, Montgomery Brown, a veteran Army Ranger. "Congratulations, Joel. I hear you've got a job with a company in northern Maine. You've earned the position. It was great sharing war stories with a combat veteran."

Joel embraced the husky Ranger. They both had experiences that only another soldier could really understand. "It was a privilege to lead such fine men. Those who never came home still haunt me."

"You're right," Monty replied soberly. "My wife understands and is a comfort, but I can't describe what it was actually like. One had to be there to really know. Will we ever be free of the memories, Joel?"

"I doubt it, Monty. Time will help. Our fraternity of brotherhood is a select group. I'm proud to be a part of it with men like you. Good luck wherever you go."

"Thanks, Joel."

Maureen and Jane saw the exchange between the two soldiers and escorted Joel to their mother. She was proud of her son. "Your father must also be proud of you, Joel. I believe he shares this day with us."

"I'm sure he does, Mother. Thanks for all the support. I could not have done it without you." He embraced her and kissed her on the forehead. "Dad was a lucky man to have won your heart."

"I won his, too," she smiled. "You're the first Thorn to go to college, son. That's an achievement to be proud of. When are you leaving for the new job with the paper company?"

"I plan to take a few days to visit with old friends at home and to prepare for a full-time position in the civilian work force. I may turn my coupe in for a new Studebaker pickup truck."

"That would be nice, dear. You should reward yourself once in a while. I sometimes worry about you. I've seen how you sit alone and stare at the walls for hours at a time," she said, straightening his necktie.

"Things have not always gone well in my private life, and I'm responsible for those shortcomings."

"I know that you haven't spoken to Inger since you transferred from New Hampshire," Maureen told him.

"How do you know that, Maureen?"

"I've spoken to her several times over the years since you two parted. She's busy teaching and usually goes to summer school to keep up with the times," Maureen answered.

"How is she doing, Maureen?"

"It's hard to tell with her. She never lets anybody penetrate that protective shield she places around her. She has never mentioned you except to wish you happiness."

His sister's description of Inger was accurate. It was her way of coping and keeping pain inside. He believed that her wish for his happiness was sincere. Just the mention of her name gave him flashbacks to the day they said good-bye. He had treated her badly. It was a guilt he could not shed.

The next day he took a trip to the coast for a few days before he left for his new job. He had heard about an author who wrote a book with the title, *MY GOD! WHERE ART THOU?* The book described a woman prison camp run by the Japanese. She was having a book signing at a bookstore in Ogunquit, Maine. Joel loved the Maine coast especially when it was relatively free of tourists. He drove the coupe to Wells and then to Ogunquit where he located the St. Aspinquid Hotel owned and operated by an old friend of the family, Mrs. Carroll. His mother and Mrs. Carroll grew up together in central Maine and had remained friends over the years.

He drove past the resort hotel to the bookstore at a pavilion near the beach. A few people were standing in line in front of the store. Joel parked the coupe and took his place in line. The author was an older woman with white hair hanging loose around her shoulders. She was tall and thin with pronounced facial bones. She graciously signed each book for the customers and thanked them. Joel was the last one in line. He picked up one of the books and glanced through it. The cover portrayed women with shrunken bodies and wide open eyes staring emptily through a barbed wire fence.

"May I sign one for you, Sir?"

"Yes, please sign it to me, Joel Thorn. The cover is realistic."

The author dedicated a book to him and signed her name. She looked at the artificial limb and then stared at him, making him uncomfortable. "Are you the Major Thorn who freed a POW camp on Luzon?"

The question surprised him as he was taking money from his wallet with his tongs. "Yes, I was one of many," he answered.

"It can't be," the lady cried excitedly. "Do you remember a 'Miss Joan' who was at the camp?"

Suddenly, the name Miss Joan with the white hair and deep-set eyes filled his memory. "Now I remember you, Miss Joan."

She leaped from the table and embraced him warmly. She was crying as she laid her head against his chest.

"Now I know why I had such a strong desire to make this trip. What a small world. So this is your story, Miss Joan."

She released him and wiped her eyes. "Yes, and many who did not survive the abuse at the camp. I owe you my life, Major Thorn. If you had been a day later, I would have killed myself with pleasure to end the misery. Since our return home, I've been determined to tell our story so that it can never happen again. I'm so glad you came today, Major. You've gladdened my heart."

"Dear lady, you've opened up a part of my consciousness that I had laid to rest. What a coincidence. I would never have recognized you."

"I have a very dear friend who helped me write the book and insisted on remaining anonymous. Would it be asking too much for you to meet with us at your convenience?"

"It would be my pleasure, Ma'am. You name the time and place," Joel replied.

"I still remember the portions of the C-rations you and your men distributed to us. It was the first food we had in days. It was the sweet taste of freedom. May I have the honor of treating you to a meal this evening?

I'm staying at the St. Aspinquid Hotel just up the street from here."

"The owner, Mrs. Carroll, is a dear family friend. I look forward to meeting you there. You've made my day. Thank you."

She embraced him again. "I will always be thankful that you came in our hour of terror. Thank you, thank you. Until tonight, Major."

"Until tonight, Miss Joan."

Meeting the unforgettable Miss Joan was an emotional shock to Joel. He remembered her as an undernourished inmate at death's door. She and the others had faced depravity and inhumanity on a scale few could imagine. He hoped that her portrayal of conditions they existed under for years would be an example of courage under adverse conditions and would never be allowed in the civilized world again.

He drove around Ogunquit, including picturesque Perkins Cove, for a few hours, then returned to the hotel. He recalled when he was about ten or eleven he had helped his father to paint the outside of the hotel. He had the job of painting the windows and sash. It was a frustrating job, but his father had told him he was a better painter for that kind of work. Joel smiled. His dad was a great guy to be with, and he treasured every moment of his childhood.

Mrs. Carroll was a very kind and caring lady. She had treated the workers to coffee and lemonade during the hot days of summer. She was a short, energetic lady who managed the facility alone. Her husband had abandoned her for a younger woman.

Joel entered the hotel through the front entrance. Mrs. Carroll was at the front reception desk and recognized him. "Joel Thorn, what a surprise. It's been years since I've seen you. Your mother has kept me abreast of your performance and injuries during the war. We're so proud of you." She came around the desk and embraced him.

"It's great to see a familiar face, Mrs. Carroll. You look as youthful as ever." He smiled at her. She was a good sport and fun to be with.

"Flattery will get you anything," she laughed.

"I stopped by to get a signed book from Hope Larsen. It's strange, but my parachute unit was the one that liberated the POW camp she was in. You would not believe how bad the inmates were when we arrived. She did not weigh a bit over eighty pounds. Every one of them was close to death. Blindness from starvation was rampant. Her eyes would have made anyone cry for justice. I told her I'd meet her here for dinner."

"She's a wonderful person. She has rented a room from me every year since the war. As a matter of a fact, she told me to direct you to the dining room. You know where it is," she pointed to her left. "I insist that this tab be on the house. Welcome home, soldier. Your sacrifice for our country is truly appreciated. If I do not see you again, give my best to your wonderful mother."

"I sure will, Mrs. Carroll," he said, kissing her on the cheek.

The dining room was partially filled with patrons. He spotted Miss Joan sitting at a table near the large window with a view of the beach. "Mrs. Carroll said you were in here."

"I'm so glad you came. Please sit down," she said with a smile. "Is it proper to call you "Major," or may I use a less formal title?"

"Please call me "Joel," and I'll call you Hope, with your permission. It's a lovely name. The world will never know the 'Miss Joan' that I knew. Perhaps your book will change that. I'm looking forward to reading it. It took courage to write about such a personal tragedy. I applaud your efforts."

"You're a kind man, Joel. Oh," she exclaimed, looking over his shoulder across the dining room. "Here comes my friend I mentioned to you." Hope left her seat to embrace the woman as she reached the table. Joel stood up and turned to greet the visitor, receiving the shock of his life. There beside the table was Inger!

Suddenly, he felt weak in the knees and was speechless. She was equally alarmed. There was hesitation in her eyes. Should she leave or sit down?

"Inger, I want you to meet the soldier who liberated our prison camp on Luzon, Major Thorn. Major, this is my dear friend, Inger Williamson."

It was an awkward moment for both of them. Joel found his voice first. "Hello, Inger. It's been a while."

"You appear out of the blue, what a surprise, Joel. Hope has talked often about the soldier who freed the prison camp. I remember thinking it might have been you, but dismissed it as improbable."

"You two know each other," Hope stated firmly. "Do I detect hesitancy? Have I made a mistake in bringing you two together? If that is so, I apologize for the poor judgment. I was simply anxious to share with Inger the joy of once again meeting a very brave soldier who inspired all of the inmates to want to live again."

"We're from the same town, Hope. We graduated from the same class in high school. If Inger doesn't mind, I'd be honored to have dinner with two very lovely ladies who have been a part of my life. Yesterday is history, and we can't do anything to change it, even if we had a chance. Today is a new day that I'd like to share with you two," He looked at Inger and had to fight his impulse to take her into his arms. She was dressed in a light green pant suit with a dark green blazer and beret positioned at a rakish angle on her head. Her hair was pulled behind her ears and fell loose about her shoulders.

Inger replied with moist eyes, "I'd like that, too. I thought that coupe might have been yours in the parking lot. You're looking well. Congratulations on your graduation from Orono."

"Thanks, Inger. It was a struggle, but I made it."

Hope calmly evaluated her two guests. "Now my senses tell me that at sometime, somewhere, you two had a more than casual relationship. I won't pry, and I want you both to know that I can be very discreet when the occasion warrants it."

"You're a perceptive lady, Hope Larsen. A few years have passed since Inger and I parted. I'd like to think that I've matured since then. I can tell you from experience that to call Inger Williamson a friend is a privilege shared by few, because she wisely chooses her friends. She's a beloved teacher in our small town high school."

Hope placed a hand on Inger's arm. "I attended her night classes in creative writing on the advice of an old friend. Our Inger is a very private person, and she's a gifted teacher who inspires excellence."

"Your description of her is correct."

"Please stop," Inger cried aloud, embarrassed by the compliments. "Both of you are making me feel uncomfortable. I came here today to celebrate a courageous lady's success as an author. I wanted to pay tribute to someone who has witnessed more human depravity than anyone I know, and has portrayed it with sensitivity and compassion. It is I who am proud to call her a friend. Now, at the same time, I meet an old friend of many years who played a pivotal role in my friend's survival. I'm overwhelmed."

"As you two know, Mrs. Carroll is an old friend who has insisted on picking up the tab for tonight's celebration. Shall we order, ladies?"

Chapter Twenty

Towards the end of a wonderful meal that met all of their expectations, Joel made a confession. "It was nice to share some time with you two without feeling guilty. When I lost my arm, I was depressed and considered myself an incomplete human being. I can share honestly with you that those feelings paled in comparison to the regret I've harbored since I walked away from Inger."

Hope heard him correctly and looked at Inger for her reaction. Normally Hope did not get involved in other people's affairs, but these two unique individuals had become a part of her life, and she was concerned about what had transpired between them.

Inger knew the statement was aimed at her, and she was unprepared to discuss the issue in Hope's presence. "Every human being has regrets and things in their past they would like to change. Decisions that are made in a state of anger can often be dismissed as unimportant. Those that are made with full recognition of the consequences are usually correct. If they prove to be wrong, that does not mean the premise used to make the decision was wrong."

His decision to choose Athena over Inger was being interpreted by her as correct. He was confused and wished he had remained quiet about past relations in front of Hope.

Hope tried to make light of the situation. "Listen, you two, I don't want to be a referee in a private war, and I do not want to take sides in your disagreements. I'm older than either of you and have experienced a full life. My husband was killed in the war. For what it's worth, the only advice I can offer you is to listen to your heart. Our hearts, if truly interpreted, can never lead us astray. At some time, you two have got to sit down and talk without intruders around. Would you promise an old friend to do that?"

"I apologize," Joel conceded. "My statement was out of line and out of place."

"I also apologize for taking your statement to task." Inger turned to Hope. "As for you, dear friend, your advice is well intended, and at some time Joel and I will have that conversation we both need. I'm sorry I spoiled your day of celebration. I wanted it to be a special occasion that you'll remember for a long time."

"This has been a wonderful experience for me. If I had the power, I'd resolve any differences you two share, but all that I can think of is you must follow your hearts. True friends are a rare and precious gift that cannot be discarded lightly."

"With those words of consolation, ladies, I'll leave with best wishes for your special day, Hope. You and your companions from the prison camp will always have a distinct place in my heart. Good luck and God bless." He turned to Inger. "It was nice to see you again, Inger. Give my best to your brother. I'll be leaving the area soon for the northern Maine woods. Thank Mrs. Carroll for me. The dinner was great as usual."

He was anxious to leave the dining room and walked directly to his coupe, starting the engine as Inger rushed to him. "Please don't leave like this, Joel. I have something to tell you. Can you meet me in an hour at the Nubble Light?"

"Yes," he replied. "I'll be there. I'm sorry I spoiled the evening."

"We'll talk later," she said, returning to the dining room.

An hour later, Joel spotted her Pontiac coming up the hill to the lighthouse. She parked beside the Studebaker and took a seat beside Joel. "Have you been here long?"

"This is one of my favorite spots to reflect on where I've been and what the future holds. I can't use the lookout at Lake Holly anymore without being confused."

"Can you tell me what happened between you and Athena? If you think it's none of my business, I'll understand."

"How can I tell you what I don't know myself?" he quietly responded and proceeded to tell Inger about Donald and Athena's decision to stay with him. "After that, I transferred to Orono to complete my studies, but you probably know that."

"Yes, I knew that. Athena was not good for you. You must realize that now."

"Hindsight is always 20/20, Inger, but it doesn't stop the ache that accompanied it. The rejection was difficult and it made me feel even angrier that I had inflicted the same hurt on you," he told her.

215

"You can't imagine the bad time I had, Joel."

"I'd take it all back if I could," he cried.

She sighed. "I believe you, Joel, really I do. However, there is something I must tell you. There's a new history teacher at the high school, Tim Jones, an Army veteran of the war. We've become good friends. I grieved for a long time over what we had lost. Tim has erased that awful feeling of being discarded like an old shoe, and I don't feel alone anymore. Can you understand that?"

"I get your message loud and clear, Inger," he quickly replied. "I'm glad we had this conversation. It gives me a clearer view of the future. Thanks for being honest with me. I do wish you the very best. You deserved better than what I did to you."

"I do not hate you, Joel. I was terribly depressed for a long time, but I never hated you, never. I pray that you will find happiness and peace of mind. You deserve that. Good-bye, old friend. Thanks for the memories."

"Good-bye, Inger," he replied, fighting the tears bursting for release.

She slowly got out of the Studebaker and got into her car. He watched her and waved good-bye. She left with a final toot on the horn. He watched her taillights until they disappeared around the corner, and wept for a long time. All he was left with were memories...

Two days later, Joel loaded up the coupe for his trip to Millinocket where he would start a new career and a new life. He embraced his two sisters, Maureen and Jane, and turned to his mother. "I'll call to let you know how I'm settled and to give you my new address, Mom.

Thanks for all the support and love. My dad was a lucky man."

She smiled and released him. "I pray that you'll find the happiness you deserve, son. Drive carefully."

"I will, Ma," he said, walking to the coupe.

He looked down the road and saw Inger's Pontiac turning into the driveway, stopping behind the coupe. She leaped out of the car and ran to Joel with tears streaming down her cheeks.

"What's wrong, Inger?" he asked.

"Everything, Joel. I can't have you leave like this. For the past two days I've analyzed everything except my heart. Hope was right, my heart still belongs to you. I never stopped loving you, never..."

They embraced for a long time and let their hearts commune with each other. "If you only knew how much I regretted hurting you, Inger. I must have been crazy out of my mind."

"Wherever you go, I'll follow you," she whispered in his ear.

"Will you marry me?'

"Oh, yes, I'll marry you..."

Other Historical Romance Novels
BY Clifton LaBree

A Song for Lisa   A Historical Romance

This is the story of a young American woman captured by the Japanese in the Philippines, 1941. Like most prisoners, she was brutalized and sadistically treated with a cruel disregard for human life. Three years later, Lisa and her companions had reached the low point of starvation and abuse .....

Lake of Three Sorrows   A Historical Romance

A warm spiritually uplifting story of courage, commitment, and sacrifice. This is the story of Dale Cooper, a battle-weary American soldier who served in two world wars.

Flickering Flame (Colonial Series Book One)

A historical novel, about the Cullen family who settled in Portsmouth, New Hampshire, and their participation in events prior to the French and Indian War. Freedom and opportunity were on the march, but it extracted a heavy price. Frontier settlers were ruthlessly killed and butchered by rampaging Indians lead by French officers and Jesuit priests who frequently incited them to greater levels of inhumanity...

Raising the Torch (Colonial Series Book Two)

A continuation of the saga from Flickering Flame, Colonial Series book one, of the Cullen family in Colonial Portsmouth. This is a moving story of love and sacrifice when a small colony had the audacity to fight for independence from their motherland...

Non-Fiction Books

By Clifton LaBree

New Hampshire's General John Stark, Live Free or Die: Death Is Not the Greatest of Evils

Publisher - Fading Shadows Imprint

A fresh look at one of America's staunchest defenders of liberty and freedom. John Stark was a courageous New Hampshire citizen-soldier who fought in both, the French and Indian War, and the Revolutionary War. His pursuit of leadership excellence on the battlefield distinguished him as one of the most successful combat commanders of the war, and one of the least appreciated.

His selflessness, modest life style, and devotion to the cause of freedom are an inspiration that time has not diminished. He remains today the embodiment of the frugal, independent, and cantankerous New Hampshire Yankee.

Gentle Warrior, General Oliver Prince Smith, USMC

Published by - Kent State University Press. Kent, Ohio, 2001

The Story of one of the United States Marine Corps best General Officer. His flawless performance in Korea is a story that needed to be told.

FADING SHADOWS IMPRINT

Fading Shadows Imprint was established to bring to the public books of historical events and portraits of people enduring tragic circumstances of by-gone days. Hopefully, they will generate a deep appreciation and respect for the exceptionalness of the United States of America, and an appreciation for the sacrifice and selflessness of those who valiantly served for liberty and freedom.

The characters are fictional, but the historical events and dates have been seriously researched and are factually presented. Some books feature incidents during the French and Indian Wars as well as the War for Independence.

World Wars I and II are eras rich in stories that beg to be told. I've tried to pay tribute to the collective courage and heroism, often unheralded, that has defined Americans in every engagement. It was a time when the immortality of dreams and aspirations were defended by the blood of young men and women. There is a beautiful monument and cemetery in a small French village where thousands of white crosses and Stars-of-David are set in perfect alignment, honoring thousands of American soldiers who gave their last full measure. A large granite slab bearing mute witness to their sacrifice has the following words chiseled in stone: TIME WILL NOT DIM THE GLORY OF THEIR DEEDS. Another monument reads: VIRTUE AND COURAGE ARE THEIR OWN MONUMENT AND REWARD. Those simple words define the American soldier from the dark days of the Revolutionary War to the present. They are an American treasure, unique in the history of the world.

Every generation has its own signature and characteristics that uniquely define them. The World War II generation is defined by the immortality of the ideals and truth they gallantly defended.

The United States has freely given precious blood and treasure to defend the rights of man to be free, and we have never asked for anything in return. No other nation on the planet has sacrificed so much for the noble virtues of liberty and freedom. We hope that the selections offered by Fading Shadows Imprint will touch your hearts and generate a deeper appreciation and love for our country.

www.ingramcontent.com/pod-product-compliance
Lightning Source LLC
Chambersburg PA
CBHW072237170626
46813CB00003B/1263